IRENE HARRINGTON

THE
APPLE TREE

THE APPLE TREE
Copyright © 2020 by Irene Harrington
ISBN 978-1-7345235-5-3

Designed & Published by King's Daughter Publishing
Indian Trail, North Carolina 28079
www.KingsDaughterPublishing.com

Printed in the United States of America.

DEDICATION

This book is dedicated to my grand girls: Jazmine Harrington, McKenzie Harrington, Kimora Harrington, Kalisha Harrington and Kendolyn Harrington. Thank you, Jazmine, for giving me that extra push to express my feeling in books. You always encouraged me when I said, "No more books." To you McKenzie, you are a very smart young lady. You helped me with words of wisdom when I didn't have words of my own. Kimora, you wanted more from each book I wrote. You had questions of why, when, who and you've learned so much by reading. Kalisha, you knew so much of what I was trying to say to others by reading and asking questions. Kendolyn, you will grow up and learn to read all the books on your own. You have heard stories told about your grandparents and great grandparents. Always keep them in your heart.

To my grandsons: Kelvin Harrington, Jr. and William T. Wall, the only young men in the family. Learn what family really means. Family matters and should always be highly valued. All my books are part of your family history. I have left a legacy for all of you to follow. I encourage you to dream dreams that will please you and your God. When I have departed from this earth, tell your families about me. Let then know that you had a Mema who loved you all every much.

~ IRENE HARRINGTON

FOREWORD

It is a good thing to be given the opportunity and ability to look back on my parents' lives and reflect on the different things that happened in our neighborhood. Having this chance to relive these precious moments of my Dad and Mom will always be in my heart.

This book is about how one man exercised his faith in prayer, understood God's expectations of him, and displayed the great love he had for his family and friends. My father taught us to value what God has created and that if we listen to God, life will be much easier. We only have a limited time on this earth. The legacy we leave behind should be to follow Christ in our daily walk of life.

I pray that this book will help you on your Christian journey with your neighbors, friends, and family members. Most of all, I hope it will help you obey the will of God. The Bible declares there's joy for those who follow the advice of the Lord. We should meditate day and night on His Word. We will be like that tree planted by the riverbank, bearing fruit each season. Its leaves never wither, and they will prosper in all they do (Psalm 1:1-3).

I pray that this book helps you leave a legacy that would lead your family to Christ in prayer.

~ IRENE HARRINGTON

THE OLD APPLE TREE

TABLE OF CONTENTS

CHAPTER I

As the day began in this small town of Anson, people would gather at the old corner store. Mr. William was a regular customer. All his family and friends called him "Will." He often went to the store to buy seeds for his garden. Will and his wife, Olivia, had ten children, who were now grown and had moved to other surrounding cities in the state.

While searching for what he needed, he always had time to chat with his friend, Mr. Sowell. Everyone knew him as "Edward." These two buddies grew up together, and at the age of 18, they both joined the military—Mr. Will joined the Navy and Mr. Edward, the Army.

Now that they had retired, there wasn't too much to do nor a place for entertainment. Most of their friends were dead, and their wives were busy keeping the house, visiting the county rest homes and doing missionary work for their church.

Every summer, Mr. Parker plowed the fields and made sure all the soil was clear of large rocks and debris. He was never in a rush. He took his own sweet time to get the job done. It was Mr. Will's time to get his garden plowed. He watched Mr. Parker for hours. He knew what length and width he wanted the garden, and no one could change his mind. "Man, don't go too far down that hill," he warned Mr. Parker. "Watch out for that hole—a water pump was there long years ago. I don't want you to get stuck out there," he said.

The garden was finally ready for planting seeds. Mr. Will always planted squash, tomatoes, okra, cucumbers, and red peppers. One of his grandsons would help plant the seeds. Separating the seeds was a big job. One row at a time and two rows for each vegetable. It took him a week to plant all his seeds.

Mr. Will's dog, Snow, walked back and forth to the garden spot. "Snow, don't you walk in my garden. Did you hear me?" he asked. That dog would look at Mr. Will as though he understood everything he said.

If Mr. Will said, "Come," the dog came. If he said, "Stay," the dog didn't move. It was amazing how an animal could obey a demand, and some people can't make their children come in for dinner.

Mr. Will loved that dog. He would buy the best dog food and would take him to the vet for a bath and to get his yearly shots.

Snow walked away from the garden. He laid on the porch. There were three dogs in the neighborhood. Snow watched the dogs run up the street, then looked back at Mr. Will to see what he was doing. When he got a chance, he ran with his buddies and didn't return. All morning long, Snow didn't come back home.

The next day, before watering his garden, Mr. Will felt ill. His wife noticed that he wasn't himself. "Pa, are you alright?" she asked. He walked into the house and sat in his favorite chair. "Pa, what's wrong? Do you want to go to the doctor?" she asked again. Mr. Will didn't answer. He just nodded and sat quietly with his hand under his chin.

A few moments later, his son drove up. "Hey, hey, hey, I'm coming in! What's wrong with him?" his son asked. "Daddy, are you alright?" Mr. Will was silent. He didn't raise his head or answer his son. "Mom, I think we should take Dad somewhere," said their son. "He's been like that since after twelve," said Mrs. Olivia. Where do you want to take him?" she asked. "Monroe is the nearest and the best hospital." their son replied.

Mr. Will's wife gathered his personal belongs, and off to the hospital they went. When they arrived at the hospital, the nurses examined Mr. Will. He didn't have a fever, nor did he appear to be in pain. The doctor entered the room. He looked at Mr. Will and asked, "What's wrong, my friend?" Mr. Will began to cry.

"I really don't think there's anything physically wrong with him," the doctor said. "If I had to guess, I would say, his heart is broken. Something has happened to cause it, but what? Has anyone died lately—a close friend, a relative, or his pet?" he asked. His wife looked at the doctor in despair, and said, "I haven't seen his dog, Snow, since yesterday. Pa, has Snow been outside with you today?" Mr. Will looked at his wife as tears streamed down his face. "Oh, my Lord, that's what it is. I haven't heard him call that dog this morning," said his wife.

"What we can do is let him stay here for a day or two and watch him," said the doctor. "He is suffering from a sickness called 'loneliness.' If not treated properly, he could go into a depression stage that would cause some serious damage to his brain. Things will get better when we find the dog or find out what happened to him. For your sake, Ma'am, I hope this pet of his isn't dead," said the doctor.

The next day, everyone in the neighborhood heard the news about Mr. Will and his dog. Some of Mr. Will's friends gathered at the picnic table in his front yard. They came from all over. They all decided to go on each street and look in wooded areas, behind the neighbor's back yards, and search the parks and highways. They walked for miles. There was no sign of Snow.

On the third day, Mr. Will was still in the hospital. The nurse helped him with his bath and changed his clothes. "Did they find my dog?" he asked the nurse. "No sir, but they will! Don't you worry about your best friend," she said. "I know how you must feel. I had a puppy for 12 years, and he is resting with the Lord. You do know that dogs go to heaven too!" Mr. Will looked at the nurse and then held his head down. He got up and looked out the hospital window. "I thought I heard something. It sounds like Snow barking in those bushes across the street," said Mr. Will. "I must be losing my mind. How in the world did I let an old dog get to me like this? I'm getting too old for this. I feel so bad. I'm just an old man who doesn't have anything else to do in this old world. I let a dog make me sick. I've never been this sick where I didn't want to eat. It sounds silly, doesn't it?" he asked the nurse. She kept silent. Just being there to lend an ear was enough for Mr. Will. The doctor decided to release Mr. Will from the hospital. Mrs. Olivia agreed to take care of him and if needed, she would bring him back.

The news got out all over the town. A white dog was missing, and it belonged to Mr. Will who lived on Coley Hill. His sons decided to give a reward of $50 to the person who found the dog. Everyone in the neighborhood was out searching for Snow. They looked for a week, but no one found him.

Early Saturday morning, Mr. Will's wife heard a knock at the back door. "Who in the world is that, knocking this time of morning?" she wondered aloud. She went to the back door, and lo and behold, Snow stood at the door, covered in mud from head to toe! "Pa, get up. Come see what I found at the door," his wife cried. Mr. Will got up and walked to the door. "My God," he said. "Come here boy! Where in the world have you been? Did you get in a fight? Look at your ears and neck. I got to call my baby, so we can give him a bath. I sure would like to take him to the vet if they're not closing early today. Honey, call the police station and let them know that Snow made it back home," said Mr. Will. He went outside and gathered all his things to work on Snow. He got his tin tub, antiseptic, shampoo, and some gloves. He had to be careful because Snow's cuts seemed to be deeper under his mane. He put Snow in the warm water and gently rubbed him.

Later, his son drove up. "Daddy, where did you find him?" he asked. "I didn't," Mr. Will said. "He came home this morning. Your momma heard something knocking at the door early this morning. She opened the door, and there he was, standing there as muddy as can be. I want to take him to the vet, but I think we need to clean him up first. You hold him while I bathe him and put this medicine on him. I'm going to feed him and give him some water. He'll be alright in a few days. Let everyone know that he is home now," said Mr. Will.

"You know what, son? A dog is just like a man," said Mr. Will. "The Bible relates us to dogs. I can't tell you what book of the Bible it's in, but it's in there. A man will go out in the streets and stay for hours. The wife doesn't know where he is, and can't find him, either. Whenever he comes back home, he's all beat up, cut up and messed up. Sometimes, he will get in a fight. He's doing something he shouldn't be doing. When he comes home, some women will accept him back, and some women won't. That's the way life is for some men. I don't want to be like that, and don't want you living like that either," said Mr. Will.

Mr. Will had always been a spiritual man. He read his Bible daily, and knew what God expected of him when it came to the land and animals in this world. He loved to read the book of Genesis. He could tell his family some amazing scriptures about what God wanted us as humans to do.

A Few Hours Later

Edward drove his old pick-up in Mr. Will's back yard. He walked to the front door. He peeped in the door, and saw Mrs. Olivia standing at the kitchen sink. "Anybody home in here?" he yelled as he opened the door to let himself in. "Come on in if your nose is clean," said Mrs. Olivia as she smiled at him. "Is Will here?" he asked. "Yes. He is on the other side of the house talking to my baby about that dog," she said. "You can go out the side door. You know Snow came home this morning!" she said happily.

Edward looked at her and smiled as he walked outside to find Mr. Will. "Hey man. Come on 'round and sit for a while," said Mr. Will. "My dog came home, and it really feels good to hold him in my arms again," he said. Edward reached in his back pocket and pulled out a pack of tobacco and bit a plug. Then, he sat down in one of the lawn chairs. He watched as Mr. Will rubbed and gave his dog some love.

"Edward, have you ever wondered why God made animals before he made man?" Mr. Will asked. Mr. Edward looked at Mr. Will with a puzzled look. He didn't answer, but continued to chew his tobacco and waited for Mr. Will to answer. "You know what? God made the animals first, so when he made man, he would have something to do," continued Mr. Will. "That is why we should take care of the animals. God saw that he needed some help with all those creatures. He could have done it himself, but why make man? He needed to do something with his time on earth. God had already worked for six days making everything. Doesn't it sound right to you?" he asked Edward. "I don't know, Will. I read my Bible sometimes, but not enough to know all about that animal stuff," said Mr. Edward, as he nodded his head for a nap.

Mr. Will looked at his friend who was fast asleep with his head on the picnic table. "Man, you're sleep! Did you hear anything I said?" asked Mr. Will. "Oh well, nobody pays me any attention anymore. I might as well be talking to myself. Edward never reads his Bible, but one thing he is good at…making wine. That's all he wants to do nowadays. He needs to get his garden plowed before Parker goes out in the country! Those people out there will keep him for months. They raise collards and salad greens and sweet potatoes," Mr. Will said to himself.

About five minutes later, Mr. Edward raised his head as if he didn't know where he was. "Well, well, well. I just came over here to catch me a nap. I got to get up from here and go home. I'll see you later, man," said Edward as he got in his truck. The two men said their goodbyes, and Mr. Edward drove away.

Mrs. Olivia called Mr. Will in for dinner. "I'm glad that dog is home. He stayed away a long time. I bet he was on the other street with those stray dogs; fighting over a girl dog, just like some men will do over a woman," Mrs. Olivia said. Mr. Will didn't raise his head. He acted as though he didn't hear a word she said.

They sat quietly watching the news, until bedtime.

CHAPTER 2

The next day, Mr. Will had to go into town. He was looking for fertilizer for his garden. He went in the Home and Garden department at the Super-Mart. "Hello there, young man. I'm looking for some fertilizer for my garden," said Mr. Will. "I don't need a large bag, just enough for a small area in my back yard." The young man spoke to Mr. Will and continued to walk with him on Aisle 8, where the feed and seeds were. "Sir, we have this box, and it's only $7.98. Would you like one of these?" the salesman asked, holding the product for Mr. Will to examine. "I'll take that one," he said to the young man.

Mr. Will continued to walk around the store. As he walked up and down the aisles, he saw one of his old neighbors and friend, Thomas. Everyone called him "Tee." "Tee, is that you? Man, if I knew you were coming out here, I would've caught a ride with you," said Mr. Will. They shook hands, talked for a few minutes and said their goodbyes.

On the way to the parking lot, Mr. Will looked at the display on the sidewalk in front of the store and saw some apple trees. They were young apple trees, exactly right for planting. He looked at the price tag. "Granny Smith? I've never heard of a Granny Smith apple," he thought. Mr. Will saw the young man who waited on him in the store. He motioned for him to come outside and take the tag off, so he could pay for it.

Away he went with the tree on the back of his truck. When he arrived at home, his wife saw him pull up in the yard. She walked outside to see what he had bought. "Pa, what did you buy this time?" asked Mrs. Olivia. Mr. Will smiled at her and took his tree off the truck. "I'm going to plant me an apple tree. I've always wanted me some trees in the yard, but I didn't know what kind to buy. I'll get Robert to help me dig the hole for it," said Mr. Will. Mrs. Olivia looked at him and shook her head as if to say, "Here he goes again!"

Early the next morning, Mr. Will got in his truck to get Robert. He didn't have to go far, because Robert was already on his way to Mr. Will's house before it got too hot. "Hey man," Robert said. "You on your way to get me?" Mr. Will greeted him and told him to hop in the truck. As they were riding down the street, Robert didn't close and lock the truck door. When Mr. Will turned the curve, the door of the truck flew opened and Robert was hanging on for dear life! "Dog blasted, man! Why didn't you close the door good? Are you okay?" Mr. Will slowed down and waited for Robert to close and lock the door. "You know this truck is old. You going to be the cause of me killing you, and in front of my house, too!" said Mr. Will.

"Cousin, I'm alright!" said Robert. "I've fallen out of cars and trucks more than one time. God still got me, though. I'm good! What you want me to help you do, today?" asked Robert. Mr. Will pulled into his driveway. Robert helped him get the tree off the truck. Mr. Will and Robert walked to the back yard. Robert went to the barn to get the shovel and the pick. He dug a hole deep enough for the tree roots to go in. "Man, that looks good. You put it in the right spot," said Mr. Will. "It's not too close to the house and it's not too close to the clothesline. I can sit out here and watch the deer. They will eat everything I plant out here. Man, I don't know what I would do without you. I don't care when I need somebody to help around this house, I can always depend on you," said Mr. Will. He paid Robert a few dollars and drove him back home.

Saturday Morning

The boys who lived out of town would come home to see their parents every other weekend. Mr. Will was just like a child in a candy store when they were home. "Come around here son, I want to show you something," said Mr. Will excitedly. "I'm going to have me a farm on this lot. I have enough room back here to plant a peach tree, a plum tree, a pear tree, and another apple tree. Look at that! I had Robert to plant this one yesterday," said Mr. Will.

His sons looked at the tree and told their dad it was nice. One of the boys wanted to buy Mr. Will whatever tree he wanted. "Dad, this is a good idea. Let me know when you're going to plant another one. I'll buy them myself. You can have a farm right here in your back yard. You could get some blueberries and raise your own fruits. This is a rich piece of property on this hill. You don't need any fertilizer because this land had a lot of outside toilets on it. I don't care what you plant on it, it's going to grow," his son said laughing.

"Who did you say dug the hole for you?" asked one of the boys. Mr. Will told him that Robert dug the hole and planted the tree. They all went inside the house and discussed getting more trees to plant.

Later that Evening

"You know Momma, the Bible doesn't lie. In the book of Genesis, God talked about the tree of good and evil. It didn't say what fruit that tree bore, but I believe to my soul, it was an apple tree," said Mr. Will. "If you look at the apple tree, it has a different appearance than all the other fruit trees. Have you noticed how beautiful they are in the spring of the year?

They have beautiful apple blossoms and they smell so good. You know another thing? The woman saw that the tree was good. She knew that it was going to be something exciting to eat. She couldn't help it. I bet those apples were different colors, shining so pretty, big and round, hanging on its own limb, all by themselves. Women always look for beautiful things. They will go miles for something pretty. They like beautiful clothes, beautiful furniture for the house, beautiful curtains and towels. I'm telling you now, just leave it to a woman to find something pretty. You see how they ran after me! I was a beautiful man—good to look at. My hair was black and wavy. My skin was like butter. Yes sir, I was one fine looking man and you knew I was!"

Mr. Will's wife looked at him and smiled, "Pa, it's time for you to go to bed."

CHAPTER 3

Sunday Morning

Mrs. Olivia woke up at her usual time—5 a.m. on the dot! She made breakfast for her husband and washed the dishes. "Come get your breakfast and drink your coffee while it's hot, Pa. I'll make the bed later. Pa! Do you hear me calling you? Lord, where in the world is that man?" asked Mrs. Olivia. She looked in all the bedrooms. She looked in the bathroom. "Jesus! Don't let me find that man laid out for dead," she said to herself. Finally, she looked out the kitchen window, and there he was! Mr. Will was outside kneeling down on the ground near the apple tree. Mrs. Olivia walked out on the porch. She heard him praying:

"Lord, I just want to thank you for all my blessings. You gave me this house and then Lord, you gave me 10 beautiful children. You didn't have to bless me the way you did, but I am so thankful. I've never been a good man. But you said in your word, 'There's no one perfect but the Father.' I want to ask you for a special blessing. I planted this apple tree with love in my heart. It will always stand tall and strong. As it grows older and produces the fruit of its kind, so will I grow older and produce the fruit of my kind. This tree will have many limbs. I can see my children, my grandchildren, great-grandchildren, and my great-great grandchildren as limbs on this tree. I know this tree will be here for many generations. I want you to bless this tree for my children. No matter how old it gets, they are to never cut it down, without planting another tree from its seeds. Lord, you have never failed me yet. You made away for me to go all over the world in World War

II. I asked you to let me come back home to my family, and you did. I know there's nothing too hard for you. I'm getting up in age, Lord. Please grant me this prayer. Bless this tree! Bless every limb, every leaf, every hand that had something to do with planting it. Bless it for many years to come. In your name I pray. Amen, Lord!"

Mrs. Olivia stood over her husband as he sincerely prayed. She helped him get up. "Come on, Pa. I have your food on the table," she said. They both walked to the house with one helping the other.

It was time to get ready for church. Mr. Will took his shower, and Mrs. Olivia laid his clothes on the bed. She always wanted him to get dressed first because it took him a little longer.

10 a.m. Sunday Morning

Leaving the house for church was a challenge. Mr. Will always wanted to drive. It was his car and he made sure his wife knew the importance of the man driving his wife, instead of the other way around. He opened the car door for her. They didn't have too far to go, so putting on the seat belt wasn't necessary. Mrs. Olivia made sure he put it on anyway.

Sunday school was one of Mr. Will's favorite services. He loved answering questions that were asked by their teacher. He always gave generously for the support of the church. "I'm going to give extra this morning, Pastor. God has been so good to me. I want to be good to Him," said Mr. Will. He reached in his pocket and searched for a few dollars. He looked in his pants pockets and then his shirt pocket. "I thought I had a $5 bill in my pocket," he said as he looked at his wife. "Honey give me a five. I thought I had a few dollars in these pants," he whispered. Mrs. Olivia gave him a look that would embarrass most people, but she handed him the money and shook her head.

After Sunday Service

Mrs. Olivia cooked her Sunday meal on Saturday night. The only thing she had to do was heat and serve it. Sunday evenings were quiet and relaxing for these two. Some of the children would call and some would come by for a visit. Mr. Will always enjoyed seeing his boys. He loved the girls, but there was something special about all his tall, handsome boys, pulling up in the driveway with their nice trucks and cars. He shared a lot about himself that they could relate to. The main subject was his friends and what they did in the old days for entertainment.

As the closing of day was approaching, they gathered in the living room with their children. "It's praying time! Let us all hold hands in love and say the prayer," Mrs. Olivia said, as they all bowed their heads. The boys hugged and kissed their parents goodbye. Mrs. Olivia watched them until they all drove away.

"I love all my children," said Mr. Will. "No matter what they did and what they're going to do. God is so good to us. Sometimes, I just sit and wonder why He allowed us to have such a blessed family. It's nothing we've done so special. It makes me want to cry sometimes. I just get filled up inside," he said as Mrs. Olivia took his hand and led him in the house. She told Mr. Will to get ready for bed. She knew if she didn't, he would fall asleep in his chair, and be there all night long.

CHAPTER 4

Monday Morning

I t was time to get up! 6 a.m. on the dot. No need to shave. He was going to be busy most of the day. "Honey, have you seen my tool-box?" Mr. Will asked his wife. He searched in his barn. He looked in his storage room that was in their house, but the tools were not there. "What do you need with tools, Pa? I thought you was going to dig holes for your plants," she said. Mrs. Olivia walked to the back yard to see what he needed. "I found them. I don't know how I missed them," he said.

Mr. Will worked in his garden all morning, and half that evening. He had to finish what he started before Wednesday evening. "Come in, Pa! You need to rest. I can see you sweating from over here. I fixed your bath water with Epsom salt, just the way you like it," said Mrs. Olivia.

They said the 6 p.m. prayer and went to bed.

Wednesday Morning

The sun was bright early this morning! It was wash day for Mrs. Olivia. She always cleaned the house and washed her sheets and changed the beds on Wednesdays. Mr. Will watched the Westerns on T.V. all morning long. "Pa, are you hungry? I got some tuna and toast if you want some, and there's fruit and tea to drink in the refrigerator," she said as she walked through the house.

It was getting late. Mr. Will went outside to feed his dog. He noticed the apple tree had new little apples on it. He pulled one of the apples from the tree. "I'm going to have a lot of apples this year. This will be my first crop. I'm going to surprise everyone," he said as he smiled and nodded.

Wednesday Night Bible Study

Mr. Will never missed Bible study. He loved to challenge the church members with questions. Mr. Chavis was his best friend for life, but when it came to the Bible, Mr. Chavis was no match for his friend, Mr. Will. They would argue about anything. If Mr. Will said the Israelites didn't ride horses to cross the Red Sea, Mr. Chavis would say they did. They would go on and on forever.

Tonight, Mr. Will wanted to discuss the apple tree in the Garden of Eden. After the prayer and a song from the members, Mr. Will opened the floor with a question. "I know we are in the Book of Matthew, but I have something on my mind," said Mr. Will. "I would like for us to discuss the tree of life tonight. I need to know more about this tree. Now, the Bible never said what kind of fruit was on this tree. All it says that it was a tree of good and evil. I believe it was an apple tree. Can somebody enlighten me about this subject, please?" he asked.

One of the women in the church raised her hand and said, "Well, my understanding is, the Lord planted the garden in Eden. I guess the garden had many fruit trees in it. It could have been a pear tree, a peach tree, or it could have been an apple tree. But it also said, God put this tree in the middle of the garden. He did that on purpose. And, you know another thing? God put two trees in the middle of the garden! You all didn't know that did you? One of the trees was the tree of life, and the other tree was the tree of the knowledge of good and evil. One was life and the other knowledge. Do you all see that? God can do whatever he wants to do," she said.

Mr. Will spoke up and said, "I read that too. But you know what? I still think it was an apple tree. There's just something about an apple tree—beautiful, like some of you women. Just beautiful! Something else I want to ask. Anybody can answer if they will. Have you ever cut an apple down its middle? I don't mean to talk this way, but it looks like a woman's body part, if you know what I mean. The apple comes in different colors; just like you women. Some apples are soft and sweet; just like some of you women again. And some of these apples are hard and sour to the taste. Don't mean to offend you ladies, but it's all in the Word of God."

The pastor stood and said, "You know my brother, man enjoyed all the fruit he wanted to eat, because he was the only one there. The Lord made the animals and the birds and sea animals, but all man did was name them. God gave him the rules. Not one time did he think of touching the tree of knowledge. That joker had it made! God planted the garden, and Man ate from the bushes and trees. Man had a good time before woman was formed. He walked around carefree. Not a worry or any concerns. And another thing, when a man gets lonely and when he's all alone, he gets a little crazy in the head. He did everything the Lord asked of him, but God didn't mean for him to be alone. You see people like that today; just leave them by themselves for a long period of time, and they will start acting crazy. Some of us don't know what to do; we can't think right, we do stupid things and think stupid thoughts. And look what Adam did! After God gave him a beautiful woman, he forgot about what God told him not to do. " The church members nodded their heads to agree.

It was time to go home. The deacon of the church locked the doors and turned off the lights. Mr. Will and his wife got in their truck. As they left the parking lot, Mr. Will said, "I don't know why some people think they know everything about the Bible. I read my Bible every day. I don't study like I should, but I read it. I get what I know straight from the Word! If you going to answer a question, at least know what you're talking about." said Mr. Will to his wife. "Who are you talking about, Pa?" his wife asked. "Just people in general. Bible study is just what it is, studying the Bible together. Not one person trying to answer all the questions, and they think they are right, too." he said with an attitude.

His wife tried to console him by letting him know that it was going to be alright. People were going to be people, no matter where you go. They arrived safely at home and got ready for bed.

CHAPTER 5

The next day, it was cloudy and about to rain. Mr. Will got in his truck and rode to one of his favorite stores. Barrington's Hardware was a long-time hardware store that was established in the early 1950's. He and the owner had been friends ever since he worked at the White school in town. When Mr. Will walked in the store, there was another man standing at the check-out register.

"Hey, Bill! Man, I can't remember when the last time I saw you," said Mr. Will excitedly. They shook hands and stood in the store talking about old times when they worked together. "Have you started your garden yet?" Mr. Will asked. "No, man. I'm going to wait until it gets a little cooler," said Mr. Bill. "You know, I plant sweet potatoes doing this time of year. I raised some sweet potatoes as big as your head last year. And you talk about good! They were so sweet, you didn't have to add but a cup of sugar for every two pies. I made over 20 pies last year and gave them all away to my friends and church members. So, what are you getting into these days?" asked Mr. Bill.

Mr. Will stood with his hands in his pockets. He couldn't wait until Mr. Bill finished what he was saying. "Well my friend, I'm planting apple trees in my back yard. I planted my first tree about six weeks ago. It was over six feet tall when I bought it. I can't wait to eat the apples from it! I'm going to tell you something. It had to be the Lord to direct me to that apple tree. I saw the trees at the store, and in a few minutes, I knew that I was going to plant apple trees," said Mr. Will.

Mr. Bill smiled at Mr. Will as he talked about apple trees. "Man, we are going to be in business. You make apple pies and I make potato pies. And you know what, people don't mind paying for them either. I get $5 a pie. Some people give me $8 for one!" Mr. Bill said. They stood in the store laughing and talking about the good old days at work and how they were going to bake pies. Mr. Will said his good-byes and Mr. Bill got into his car and drove away.

When Mr. Will got home, he told his wife who he saw at Barrington's store. "I tell you something, that Bill can grow some sweet potatoes! He looks well for his age, too. He told me that he sold his pies for $5 each. That boy made some money! If he can do it, so can I," said Mr. Will. His wife gave him all her attention while he was talking and added, "Well Pa, all you got to do is put butter, sugar, vanilla flavor, one egg, cinnamon, and nutmeg in your potatoes and bake them in a pie shell. I think Bill whips his potatoes with his hand. I can't see him using a mixer. His potatoes are so smooth and sweet, and there's no lumps in them either," his wife said smiling.

Mr. Will was thinking as his wife spoke. The ideas were flowing in his head. He thought about doing research on apple trees. He wanted to have all the knowledge he needed to grow the best apples ever. "I know what I'll do, I'm going to pray about this thing first. I'm going to ask the Lord to lead me with this project. I wonder, how many times the Bible tells us about fruit? It's got to be in there," he said to his wife.

Mr. Will took an evening nap. While he was resting, his wife gathered all their old Bibles and dictionaries. She wanted to make sure he knew all he needed to know about apples.

The Next Evening

Mr. Will had a visitor. It was his son, who lived in the mountain area of North Carolina. He also loved planting trees in his yard. When he drove in the driveway, Mr. Will got up to see who was coming. "Lord, that's my boy! Hey son, come on in!" They grabbed each other and hugged like they hadn't been in touch in years.

"Hey, Pops! Just coming back from Tennessee. I had to take care of some business there. I bought you something, Pops! I got these trees from the mountains. They bloom year-round. You don't have to plant them; I'm going to plant them for you," said his son. They both went outside. His son dug two holes and planted the trees in the front yard. Afterwards, they went in the house, and their son hugged and kissed his mom. As he got in his car and was driving away, his mom stood on the porch waving her hand goodbye.

Later that Night

Mr. Will had to have his favorite dish—ice cream and a small piece of sweet bread. His wife was so patient and kind to fix it just the way he liked it; cake in the bottom and ice cream on top. The T.V. had to be on the evening news, and right before bedtime, he had to see his Westerns.

The Next Day

The morning time prayer was said together at 6 a.m. sharp. A good wash-up was all that was needed because Mr. Will always got in the tub at night. "Where are you going so early, Pa?" his wife asked. "I'm going out here and check on my garden. I thought I saw some small apples on the tree."

His wife looked at him and was amazed about what she heard. "Apples so early? He just planted the tree six weeks ago. That man can't sit still for a minute. He's got to be doing something all the time," she said, smiling to herself.

In that same hour, Mr. Will ran to the side door and yelled, "Honey! Come here and look! I told you there were apples on this tree! My eyes didn't fool me. I'm going to have apples this spring. I going to buy two more trees later, but not now. I'll just settle for the one I have and tend to it. I want to make apple pies first, and later next year, apple jacks, apple butter, and I'm going to ask Edward if he knows how to make apple wine," he said.

His wife came outside to see for herself. "You're right, Pa! I see a few apples. You need to leave the tree alone so it can grow," said Mrs. Olivia. "You keep looking at it! Leave it alone, the tree knows when to bear fruit. I hope the deer doesn't eat them before we get some. You remember, they ate all your squash and tomatoes last year. Leave it to Mr. Will!" she continued. "He's going to make everything with one apple tree. Lord, you got to help this man of mine."

Mr. Will walked back to the house and got his Bible. "I'm going to see what the Lord has to say about apple trees" said Mr. Will. "I know it's in here. I'll just keep reading and take my own notes. This is going to be good for me at my age. I need to learn more about what the Word says. I know about Moses, David, and Noah. I like the Old Testament! You can get more knowledge about the beginning of man. I like the part where God put us in charge of everything. Man to man, that's the way God wanted it to be," he said.

Mr. Will got his Bible and turned it to the book of Genesis. "Here is something! The first chapter and the 11th verse. God said, 'Let the land sprout with vegetation, every sort of seed-bearing plant, and trees that grow seed-bearing fruit.' This is it, right here!" he read with excitement. "These seeds will then produce the kinds of plants and trees from which they came," said Mr. Will. He closed the Bible. He looked at his wife and said, "Honey, you know what that means? The tree that I planted will never die. Years and years from now, it will look like it's dead, but there will be life in it. I can take the seeds from that tree and save them, then replant those seeds and they will produce more trees." He was excited about the good Word he read from the Bible.

Weeks Later

Lo and behold! The tree is loaded with young apples. Mr. Will got up early one morning. His wife watched him as he prepared for his project. "Will, do you have an apple pie recipe?" asked Mrs. Olivia as she washed the breakfast dishes. "No, I don't need a recipe. I know how to make a pie," said Mr. Will. "I made pies when I was a young boy. My grandma made all kinds of pies when we were little. I keep my recipe in my head. Can't nobody steal them from me there. I think I have everything I need—flour, sugar, eggs, cinnamon, and lemon juice. I don't know how to make the crust, so I'm going to the store and buy some. I want to make ten pies today. I need twenty pie crusts," he said to his wife. She looked back at him and shook her head.

Mr. Will got his keys. As he stepped into the truck, his wife came to the door and yelled, "Pa, you got enough money?" He nodded and drove away.

Later That Afternoon

Mr. Will and a few of his friends started picking apples from the tree. Edward pulled apples from the limbs and put them in his shirt tail. "I have over two dozen apples in my shirt!" he said. Robert only picked about a dozen and put them in his bucket. "Man, I didn't know it was this many apples on this tree," he said to Mr. Will.

After they gathered all the apples, Mr. Will got a tin tub and poured water in it. The three men put all the apples in the tub and sat down to see how beautiful they looked in the water. "Guys, I sure appreciate you all for helping me today. The Bible says, 'Two people are better than one, for they can help each other to succeed,'" said Mr. Will. "Where did you get that from, Will?" asked Robert. "I read it in the Bible somewhere. You know, I do read my Bible. It might not look like I do, but I do. The Bible is going to teach me about apples. You ought to read for yourself. You can learn a lot of stuff," Mr. Will said, as he washed the apples and lay them out to dry.

"The Lord is good to me. I can just cry sometimes. If it weren't for you boys and my family, I don't know what I would do. I thank you guys from the bottom of my heart," Mr. Will said.

Edward and Robert looked at the picnic table and didn't say a word. Their hearts were heavy. They knew they were going to be a part of their friend's great success story. They watched Mr. Will's every move until all the apples were clean and dry.

That Evening

Mr. Will got his Bible and a sheet of paper. He turned his Bible to

Genesis again. "The Lord God made all sorts of trees grow up from the ground, trees that were beautiful and that produced delicious fruit. That's Genesis 2:9," he read aloud. He and his wife sat quietly in the den.

"Honey, you know what? I want to leave all my children something when I die. I don't have a lot of money and you know we don't have a lot of land. It says in the Bible that a tree will last a long time. All you need to do is save the seeds from it," said Mr. Will. "God didn't mean for us to live in this world for something and die for nothing. We have a purpose here. I'm a man. I was made first. I was given the rules on how to take care of animals and the land. You know, I love dogs and I love to work the grounds. I want to do my part while I'm here. No one will never say Ol' Will lived and died without leaving his children nothing. And if my children are smart, they will teach their children the same lesson. A man got to be a man—not any kind of man, but a smart man. You got to stay in the Word of God to be smart. The Bible will teach you, but a man must be willing to study the Word," he said to his wife.

"Pa, you're not giving the woman any credit. God put us here to help man. You got Robert and Edward helping you. I can do something. I know how to peel apples and pick them too," said Mrs. Olivia as she mended the holes in his socks. "I'll let you know when I need your help," said Mr. Will. "You got things to do in the house. I don't want you to overdo it. When it's time to make the pies, you can watch them while they're in the oven. We're going to have a lot of work with freezing the pies. I want to make enough to give all the children when they come home," Mr. Will said, as he put his Bible away for the night.

CHAPTER 6

The Next Day

Mr. Will and his wife awoke early. She prepared breakfast and did her regular routine around the house. Mr. Will made his grocery list and headed to the store. When he started his car, he said a prayer before he got on the highway. "Lord, I want to thank you for waking me up this morning. You took care of me when I didn't know how I was going to make it through. As I look back over my life, I think of the times when money was hard to come by. But, you Lord, made a way. I want to thank you with a heavy heart this morning. It's heavy because I haven't always done things right. Now, I'm an old man, and I want to do more now than I've ever done in my life. I don't know why you put this idea in my head about a tree—an apple tree of all things. I know you don't make no mistakes. So, Lord, be with me on this journey. Don't let me make a mess of these pies. Be with me Lord with this one. I'm getting ready to spend some big money for my ingredients. In Your precious name I pray. Amen Lord!"

As he got out of his car, he saw one of his church members. "Hello, there Brother! What're you doing on this side of town?" asked Mr. Will. It was Mr. James who lived on the next street over from Mr. Will. "Man, I came down here to get my grands some snacks for school. What's going on with you these days?" asked Mr. James. The two men entered the store and got grocery carts. They talked as they rolled the carts down the aisles. "I got a grocery list somewhere in my pocket. I got to make twenty apple pies before the weekend. I hope they have everything I need," Mr. Will said. He looked at his list as he walked through the store. "Will, you know what? You ought to sell some of your pies to the public. Your kids aren't going to pay for them. These kids think we suppose to give them everything we have. They have good jobs now; better than what we had when we were young. How much are your pies going for?" asked Mr. James.

Mr. Will was trying to get all the items he had on his list. He looked back at James and said, "I think we're going to sell them for $5 a pie. I got to see what my wife says about it. She might want to get two or three dollars more. She's helping me, you know," he explained to James. "That's great, man! It sounds like a good thing to do this fall. I wished I had something like that to make extra money," said Mr. James as he got his eggs and milk from the produce section. "Well, man, I'm going to get some chips and get out of here," said Mr. James. Mr. James said good-bye and Mr. Will got his items and left the store.

Later that Afternoon

A dark cloud rolled over town. Everything looked dreary. "It looks like rain, Honey. I thought the weatherman said it was going to rain tomorrow. I wanted to pick some more apples today. Maybe, I can pick some before it gets dark," said Mr. Will. He sat in his old recliner chair and folded his arms and took a nap.

"Lord, that man always want to do something! He won't sit down and rest his mind. Look at him! Fast asleep. I hope he sleep until the moon comes out," said Mrs. Olivia.

The rain started at sundown. Mr. Will slept for the remainder of the evening. His wife watched him as she washed the dinner dishes. She put the grocery away and placed all of Mr. Will's items on the countertop and his pie crusts in the freezer. "Will, you better get ready for bed, it's almost 9 o'clock," said Mrs. Olivia. Mr. Will and his wife said their evening prayer. She helped him out of his chair. She locked all the doors and turned off the lights.

The Next Day

It was 6 a.m. sharp. Mr. Will got out of bed and heard his wife in the kitchen. The bathroom was the first place for him to go after getting out of bed. "Good morning, Honey! Has it started raining again this morning?" he asked his wife. She shook her head and asked, "Pa, do you want coffee and eggs this morning?" Mr. Will walked over to the refrigerator and got the coffee creamer and his favorite coffee cup. As he sat down at the table, he said, "Yes. I want toast, too."

After breakfast, he got a basket and walked to the back yard. He began picking up apples off the ground. The apples were big and had a yellowish green color. When the basket was full, he started pulling apples off the tree. "I bet I have a bushel or more apples off this tree. O' boy! Look at the ones on the top branches. If I had a long stick, I could get another basket full," he thought as he filled the baskets. His wife came out to help. She noticed that Mr. Will looked faint. "Are you alright Pa?" she asked. "Don't you get too hot out here."

Mr. Will picked up his basket and walked back to the porch. He had two big baskets full of apples. "Look at this! I can't wait until Edward comes over. He's not going to believe his eyes. I told him and Robert that I was going to have apples this year, but they said, 'No, the tree won't bear this year!' I knew what I was talking about. You can't beat God's giving. I'm going to continue to read my Bible, and the Lord will direct my path making these apple pies," he said to his wife.

They both went into the house. Mr. Will got his Bible and began to read from the book of Genesis again. "And the Lord said to the man. 'Since you listened to your wife and ate from the tree whose fruit I commanded you not to eat, the ground is cursed because of you. All your life you will struggle to scratch a living from it.'"

He removed his glasses and looked at his wife. "You know Honey, a man shouldn't tell his wife everything about what he's doing or when he's going to do it. Some women are very devious and cunning. You never know what a woman is thinking about, and you don't know who is whispering in her ears. God told man what to do. If he had listened to the Lord, I think this whole world would've been better off," said Mr. Will.

"Now, you take this apple tree," he continued. "It won't bear fruit every year. Every other year, this tree will be cursed. It's right here in the Word. You see all these apples! Next year, we won't see any. I believe that's the curse the Lord was talking about. It's good to read the Bible. What I'm learning, I want to share it with all my children. I want them to learn the importance of obeying the Lord. This tree will be here for a long time. I'm going to pray, that this tree is here for many years after I'm dead and gone," he explained to his wife.

CHAPTER 7

oney, are you going to help me wash the apples? I don't want you to do nothing but wash them. I'll peel and cut them in small pieces," said Mr. Will. Mrs. Olivia washed each apple and placed them in a bowl. Mr. Will cut the apples in half and then sliced them for baking. Everything was going as scheduled. His wife took the pie crusts out the freezer. They worked well together, as if they were on an assembly line. Now, it was time to put the apples in a bowl for mixing all the ingredients. They mixed the sugar, butter, cinnamon, vanilla favor and flour. Mr. Will did the tasting. Then, he filled the pie crusts with the mixture. His wife topped each pie with another crust. Finally, all the pies were ready for the oven. They placed four pies at a time in the oven.

One Hour Later

"Oh my goodness! You got to come see these beautiful pies. I hate to act like a fat frog, but I'm going to praise my pond today!" Mr. Will said to his wife as he took one of the pies out of the oven. He put all of the baked pies on the countertop. "Did you remember to get some foil? You need a large roll for all these pies," she asked, as she checked the grocery list to see if Mr. Will had everything. "Pa, I think you forgot the foil. I don't see it on your list. You go to the store while I stay here and fan the pies, I don't want the flies to take over in here," she said.

Mr. Will got his hat and off he went to the store.

On the way back, he saw his son turn into their street. "That looks like my baby boy! I believe it is," said Mr. Will as he waved at his son and followed him home. They greeted each other with a hug. "Come on in, son! You see all my pies? Your mom and I got the apples off my tree. Everybody said I wouldn't get apples this year, but I did! We picked apples for two days. Your mom did more looking than helping," joked Mr. Will.

His son just stood and enjoyed the conversation. "Did I hear somebody call my name?" said Mrs. Olivia. She walked into the kitchen, and there stood her son. "Hey baby. How long have you been here? I didn't hear you come in the house," she said. Their son sat down at the kitchen table. He talked about his family and the ride to Wadesboro, where his parents lived. "Pop, this is good for you. I'm glad you found something to do with yourself. There are so many men your age who are lonesome and don't know what to do with themselves, but I got to give it to you. I never thought you would be making pies," said his son.

It was time for them to say their good-byes. Mrs. Olivia always walked her children to the door and watched until they got out of sight. "I love my children. If I had my way, I would build another house with about twelve rooms in it and ask all of them to move back here with us. I love them just that much," said Mr. Will. Mrs. Olivia just looked at him and smiled.

It was getting late and dinner had to be prepared. "Pa, do you want your cream now, or do you want to take your bath?" Mr. Will didn't respond. He was sitting with his head bowed down to his chest. Mrs. Olivia thought he was asleep. "Pa, you hear me talking to you?" She touched him on his shoulder. He didn't answer. She called again. Finally, he answered. "Pa, what's wrong? Did you pass out?" she asked. Mr. Will looked at her and said, "What's wrong with me? I was in a deep sleep. I couldn't hear nothing. I felt like I was unconscious, or I blacked out. I think I need to get checked out by my doctor," he told his wife. "I think you should. I don't want you driving that truck and you blacking out. I'll call the doctor in the morning," she said, as she wrapped the pies and put them in the freezer.

9 a.m. the Next Morning

Mrs. Olivia called the doctor and got an appointment for her husband. They were to be at the doctor's office at 2 p.m. She had to start early helping Mr. Will get ready, so she made him coffee and a piece of toast. "Hurry Pa, we don't want to be late. Get your shoes and don't forget your belt. Do you have your wallet with your insurance and I.D.?" she asked. Mr. Will just watched his wife as she raced around the house trying to get him ready. "Baby, stop rushing me! We'll get there on time. I feel like there's something wrong with my insides. I can't explain the feeling, but I'm not okay," he said.

Mrs. Olivia walked Mr. Will to the car. She made sure he wore his seat belt. They got to the office in 20 minutes. They were the first patients there. It was 1:45 p.m. when the receptionist called Mr. Will's name. "Do you have your I.D. and insurance information, Sir?" she asked. Mrs. Olivia gave her the cards and followed Mr. Will to the examining room.

One Hour Later

Mr. Will was sick. He had cancer. The doctor told him he had to have an out-patient surgery and go to another center for radiation therapy. The ride back home was long and silent. There wasn't much to say.

"Pa, you got to put everything in God's hand," said Mrs. Olivia. "He knows all about us and there's nothing too hard for him. I'll call the children and let them know," she said, as they got out the car. She helped him into the house. He sat in his favorite chair. "Well, I'm glad I made my pies. If something happens to me after the surgery, you give the children the pies and don't worry about selling them," said Mr. Will as he removed his shoes. "Pa, don't start talking like that," said Mrs. Olivia. "You don't know how the surgery will be. The doctor said he was going to cut the infection part off and then you take your treatment. They have modern things now, it's not like it was years ago. These doctors are smart, they know what they're doing. You just pray and leave it to Jesus," his wife said, as she helped him get ready for a nap.

Mrs. Olivia sat in a chair at the kitchen table. She got her little phone book out of her purse. She called all the girls and told them about their father. She always had a good relationship with them. Only two of the girls seemed upset about the news. The other three thought their dad would be okay with the treatment. "Dad is strong, Mother. He will be okay with the surgery. People go through that kind of stuff every day. They have good doctors now. It's not like it was in the 60's," her daughter said.

One Week Later

Mr. Will and Mrs. Olivia were ready to go. They had to travel 35 miles from their home for Mr. Will's surgery. "Baby, please don't poke on this highway. You got to keep up with the traffic. These people will run all over you," he told his wife. "You let me do the driving, Pa. I know how to drive and know how fast to go. I don't want to get a ticket coming up here," she scolded. Mr. Will didn't say a word after that comment. He was nervous about the procedure. He didn't know what to expect.

As Mrs. Olivia pulled in the parking lot, Mr. Will told her to park near the entrance. They got out of their car and went in the hospital. As they started down the hallway, they heard someone calling their names. "Mom, Dad, wait for me." It was their baby daughter. She drove over 100 miles to give her dad support and pray with them. "Dad, you say a prayer before they start your procedure. You do know the 23rd Psalm, don't you?" she asked. Mr. Will didn't say a word. He just looked at her as if to say, "Yes girl, what do you think I am?"

The surgery lasted for about an hour. Mr. Will came out of surgery with a smile on his face. He stayed in the hospital for three days. On the fourth day, Mrs. Olivia held his hand and walked beside his wheelchair while the nurse rolled him to the front desk. They made their appointment to take treatments at the center.

On the way home, Mr. Will and his wife talked about his experience at the hospital. "God is good to me. I thank Him for bring me through!" he said.

Three Days Later

The treatment center was 30 miles from their home. When they arrived, a nurse with a wheelchair met them at the front entrance. She took Mr. Will to one of the treatment rooms. The treatment lasted nearly half an hour. "Pa, how do you feel, now?" asked Mrs. Olivia. "It didn't hurt that bad and I really don't like needles, but the needle wasn't that big. I thought they were going to give me the treatment going through my arm, but they put it in my side. It would've been better in my arm than in my side. But you know what? I thank God that it wasn't as bad as I thought," said Mr. Will.

Mrs. Olivia sat quietly while Mr. Will changed into his clothes. She went to the parking lot and got the car. On their way home, she drove the speed limit and didn't make any mistakes.

Finally, at Home

Dinner was ready. Mrs. Olivia put her things away and sat the table for Mr. Will. *"Lord we thank you for the food we are about to receive for the nourishment of our body. Christ sakes we ask all of these blessing in your powerful name, Amen,"* Mr. Will repeated the blessing with a bowed down head.

"The Lord is good all the time, Pa. You got to trust him all the time. No matter what we're going through. He said if you have the faith as small as a mustard seed, he will stay with us. He won't let us down. That little treatment is going to work. The doctors know a lot, but they don't know when the Lord's gone call us home. Only the Lord knows that," said Mrs. Olivia while eating her meal. Mr. Will ate his dinner and just nodded his head, as if to agree with everything she said.

A Few Hours Later

"What time is it, Baby?" asked Mr. Will. "Edward said he was coming over. I need to get him to help me do something. I want to go to the bank and get some money. These pies cost money. I got to get some more pie crusts." Mr. Will explained. "Pa, you don't need to make any more pies. Get rid of the ones you have. You going to have so many pies here, you won't have room for them all. You just going pie crazy! You need to freeze some of those apples for next year or give them to the children," said Mrs. Olivia. Mr. Will looked at her as if to say, "I know what I'm doing," but he just kept walking to the table to get his truck keys.

Off to the bank he drove. As he parked his truck, he saw Mr. Tee. "Hey man, I thought that was you!" said Mr. Will. "Come by the house before you go home. I got something to give you and your wife," he said. Mr. Tee greeted Mr. Will and said he would come over before going home.

Mr. Will withdrew $200 from his savings account. "I can't let that woman know how much I got out. She will have a fit. I declare, you just can't let these women folks know everything you're doing," he murmured to himself.

When he left the bank, he decided to go to Mr. Edward's house. Mr. Edwards was in his back yard, picking some blueberries from his garden. "Hey man! What're you doing? I need some help at the house," said Mr. Will. Mr. Edward watched Mr. Will as he picked through his berries.

"Hey Will, I need some help too! You help me, I help you," he said to Mr. Will, as they smiled at one another. "You still making pies?" he asked Mr. Will. "Yes! I need to make about a dozen more and I'll be finished," said Mr. Will. "These are going to be the best batch yet. I let these apples set out for a few days. You know, I started taking my treatment this week. I feel some kind-a-way about this treatment. I feel like my body is changing. I didn't feel like this before they told me I had cancer. There's a certain feeling when something attacks your body and you don't know what it is and what it looks like. You know what I mean?" he asked. Mr. Edward didn't have words for his friend. He never looked up at Mr. Will. His heart was overwhelmed with sorrow. Mr. Will was his best friend. What hurt his friend hurt him, also.

After picking berries, they both got into their vehicles and drove to Mr. Will's house. Mrs. Olivia was cleaning the kitchen so Mr. Will would have a prepared space for his apples. He and Edward started peeling apples and saving the skins to make jelly. They worked for several hours, peeling and cutting apples for pies and jelly. "Pa, you need some Sure-Jell for your jelly. Do you have enough sugar? Are your jars clean? I got this big pot to put the peelings in. Give me the peelings and I'll get started with the jelly," Mrs. Olivia said, as she got all of her ingredients ready.

When they were done, Mr. Edward went home. The kitchen was in a mess. Mrs. Olivia put all the leftovers away and cleaned her kitchen. They had prepared twenty more pies and two dozen pint jars of jelly. "I can't believe we did it!" said Mr. Will. "Now, we need to wrap the pies and put them in the freezer. Can you put the jelly in the closet? That's about the coolest place in the house. I have a box to put them in," said Mr. Will. After cleaning up, they got ready for bed.

The Next Day

Mr. Will and Mrs. Olivia had settled into a routine for the past 51 days. They had breakfast and then traveled to Mr. Will's treatment sessions.

Mr. Will made it! Finally, the treatments were over. No more traveling on the dangerous highway. Mrs. Olivia was relieved. Mr. Will was doing well, and the children were praising God for healing their dad.

CHAPTER 8

Two Months Later

Mr. Will and Mrs. Olivia sold all theirs pies. They made a $200 profit. People from everywhere bought Mr. Will's pies. Some paid $10 a pie, while others paid $5 for a pie and gave them a tip.

The Next Week

The weather was changing. There was nothing for Mr. Will to do now. Apple season was over. He looked out the kitchen window. "The apple tree looks dead. I can't let this happen! I got to pray and wait on God for an answer. There's a reason to wait! God won't allow me to go from season to season for no reason," he said.

Mr. Will got his Bible and sat in his chair. "Here it is, Honey. The Word says, 'They that wait on the Lord shall renew their strength; they shall mount up with wings like Eagles; they shall run and not be weary; they shall walk and not faint.' Isaiah 40:31," he said. "I'm going to be stronger next fall. I'm just that crazy enough to believe the Lord is going to strengthen me. What I want to do now is, clean off my garden spot for collard plants. I want to plant about two rows, but I'm going to give them away. I feel like the Lord want me to give something away to get more the next year," said Mr. Will.

Later that afternoon, he called his friend Mr. Parker to clean off his garden spot. He couldn't sit still. "Pa, what are you doing now?" asked Mrs.

Olivia. "I thought you called Parker yesterday. Pa, do you hear me talking to you?" Mr. Will was watching his favorite program on T.V. and didn't hear Mrs. Olivia. "Honey, what did you say? I heard you talking to me, but I was watching my program," he said as he stared at the T.V. Mrs. Olivia looked at him and shook her head as if to say, "Why bother?"

Mr. Will heard a truck in his driveway. He went outside. Mr. Parker was in the back yard unloading his tractor. "Hey, man. I thought that was you! I want you to plow eight rows out here. When you finish, just come to the door. I got your money," said Mr. Will. Mr. Parker told him he would clean the garden spot and make eight rows for the garden.

The Next Day

Mr. Will got up early. Off he went to the hardware store to buy collard plants. When he left the store, he decided to go the long way home. He noticed a funeral home sign at the street in his neighborhood. "That sign is at Robert's house. I hope my buddy isn't dead," he thought. He drove his car in their yard. Everything was quiet. He didn't see anyone at the house.

As he opened his truck door, someone in the house opened the front door. "Hey Mr. Will. Would you like to come in?" asked a young girl standing in the doorway. "No, baby. I saw that sign in the road. Who's dead?" he asked the girl. "Mr. Will, my dad had a heart attack last night. He passed away early this morning," she said with tears running down her face. "Baby, I am so sorry to hear that! Robert is my cousin. I loved that guy. He planted some of my apple trees and a weeping willow tree, too," said Mr. Will. "But, you know, we can't stay here. Everything God made must die sometimes. I'm so sorry to hear that. I'm going to miss him. You all have my blessings. Don't cry, baby. He's better off with the Lord. Your daddy wouldn't want to stay here depending on someone to take care of him. You all will be alright. I'll let my wife know about your loss. She will bring something down here for the family. Do you know when the arrangements will be?" he asked the girl. "No, sir. I will let your wife know when she comes," she said.

Mr. Will got in his car and drove off. Sitting in his truck all alone, his mind went back to when Robert was a young man. They were cousins, and he always enjoyed his cousins, especially Robert. They drank together. They visited the girls from their high school together. They played cards at the house with other friends. "Man, I'm going to miss that guy. Well, I guess it's time for us to check out of here. We're all getting older. Oh well, God gave us this life and God will take it away," he thought.

As he pulled in his driveway, Mrs. Olivia stood in the yard. She walked to the truck to help with the packages. She looked at Mr. Will and asked, "Pa, what's wrong?" He didn't say anything. He held his head in awe. She looked at him and grabbed the bags. "Robert died. I took the long way home from the store, and I saw the funeral home signs. It was at his house. I stopped in for a minute and his daughter told me he passed last night. I hated to hear that. It just did something to my insides," he said with tears rolling down his cheeks. "Well, we all got to leave here, Pa. I think Robert was sick and didn't tell anybody. He was always a little man. I don't think he ate right. Every time he came here, he had a pack of nabs and a Coca-Cola. You got to eat vegetables when you get to be a certain age. What could a drink and crackers do? I'll go down there tomorrow and take something for the family," Mrs. Olivia said, as she walked inside.

Five Days Later

Mr. Will and Mrs. Olivia got up early to get ready for Robert's funeral. The family wanted Mr. Will to give remarks during the service. They asked him to sing a solo, but he refused to sing. He told them that he didn't feel well enough to stand in front of a crowd and sing, and Mrs. Olivia agreed with him.

They left their home around noon. The funeral was at 1 p.m. Mrs. Olivia held her husband's hand as they walked inside the church. "Are you alright, Pa?" she asked, while looking in his face to see if he was okay. "Yes. I'm alright. Let's sit at the front. I might have to use the restroom. I don't want to get up during the service." They walked to the front of the chapel and sat quietly until Robert's family arrived.

30 Minutes Later

It was time for Mr. Will to make his remarks. Mrs. Olivia walked with him to the pulpit. "Good afternoon, everyone. My heart is heavy today," said Mr. Will. "I have lost a friend and a cousin. Robert was a good man. I know the Bible says that there's only one good man—and that man is Jesus. I'm not saying a good man like Jesus, because Jesus was a perfect man. When I say 'good,' I'm talking about a man you could trust. You could trust him with your yard, your tools, your dog, and even your money. Don't get me wrong. He wasn't perfect. It's a difference between good and perfect. I'm going to miss him!" Mr. Will continued.

"I would like to share something with the family. I never told anyone this, but Robert told me he was going to stop drinking, and he did! He changed his life several weeks ago. I think he knew he was going home.

We all must make our minds up to stop doing things that hurt our bodies. We got to clean up. Clean our minds. Clean our thoughts about each other. And most of all, clean our hearts," he said.

"I'm going to leave one thing with the family. 'I have fought the good fight, I have finished the race, I have kept the faith. Now there is in store for me the crown of righteousness, which the Lord, the righteous judge, will award to me on that day- and not only to me but also to all who have longed for His appearing.' Family, stay with the Lord and he will stay with you. Me and my wife will keep you all in our prayers. Thank you," said Mr. Will as he walked back to his seat. He took his handkerchief and wiped his eyes.

Later, After the Funeral

Mr. Will went to his bedroom to change his clothes. He looked at Robert's obituary. "Man, I'm going to miss you. We sure had some good times in our day. There will never be another man like you. All of us will be joining you soon. Oh well, I guess I'll put this one up for safe keeping. Maybe, in a few more years I'll take it out and read it again. Soon, I'll have a stack so big I'll need to get a suitcase to put them in. All of my friends will be long gone," he said as he placed the obituary in a small folder.

Mrs. Olivia called Mr. Will to the dining room for dinner. They discussed the funeral and how well the family held themselves together and how nice they put Robert away.

It was getting late. Mrs. Olivia cleaned the table and washed the dishes. She gave Mr. Will his favorite night cap—ice cream and cake. They both sat quietly in their recliners and watched the evening news.

"Pa, you better get up and get ready for bed. I laid your P.J.'s on the foot of the bed. You need to take a shower tonight, and don't run too much water," Mrs. Olivia said as she passed her husband a towel and bath cloth. Mr. Will was silent. He got up and did as she asked.

CHAPTER 9

The Next Morning

The sun was shining bright this morning. Birds sang in the tree-tops as the garbage man yelled, "Good morning!" to all the neighbors who were standing in their yards. Mr. Will walked to the back yard to look at the apple tree. A small limb had fallen off the tree. "Um' that's funny," he said to himself. "How did this happen? There's no reason why the limbs should be breaking off! I know that Robert planted this tree, but why did this limb fall after his death? I don't believe in ghosts, but something isn't right! I'm going to keep watching this tree for a while. I'll just put it on the deer this time!" he thought.

Mr. Will got his hoe and sacks. He was ready to work in his garden. He had enough collards to plant three rows. Snow followed him to the storage shed. All his tools were gone. He was in shock! He walked back to the house and as he opened the door to the kitchen, he saw Mrs. Olivia standing at the sink. While leaning on the door knob he asked, "Where in the world are all my tools? I put them in my box next to the door. I don't see the box nor my tools." Mrs. Olivia could hear the stress in his voice. She looked back at him and asked, "How do you think I know? I don't go out there when you're working. Robert is the only person who went in that barn, and your boys when they are home. Did you look good? You may have moved them somewhere else. Stop getting so out of shape when you can't find your stuff. You get yourself upset for no reason."

Mr. Will pulled the chair from the table. He sat down and put his hand under his chin. "I don't know why I let things like this get me so upset. I just don't like looking for my own tools. I don't like looking for nothing of mine when I know where I put them," he said. "When I read my Bible this morning, something told me that I was going to get angry today, and the Word said, 'Get angry; but sin not,'" said Mr. Will.

He looked at Mrs. Olivia and asked, "Do you think Robert borrowed my tools without asking me? I hate to think he did. I don't want to say he stole them because that's wrong to think that way about a friend." Mrs. Olivia looked at him, raised her eyebrows and said, "Pa, you can't put all your trust in people these days. You think you know a person, but you really don't know what people will do when your back is turned." Mr. Will looked perplexed. He kept silent. He got up and put his hat on. "I'm going to Robert's house," he said. "His girls will look around the house for me. I know my tools when I see them. I hate to go see them for something so petty, but I need my things," he said.

One Hour Later

Mr. Will pulled up in Robert's driveway. He knocked on the door. One of the girls answered. As she opened the door, she saw that it was Mr. Will. She asked him to come in. "Hey, baby. I hate to come down here bothering you girls, but by any chance have you all seen some tools laying around the house? Your daddy helped me plant a few trees last year and he may have borrowed my tools," said Mr. Will.

The girl looked at Mr. Will and said, "Yes sir. I saw a toolbox on the back porch. I thought it was Daddy's, so I put it in his closet. You can come in here and see if it's yours." Mr. Will followed her to the bedroom. There was a wooden toolbox on the floor of the closet. "That's it! Are all my tools in it?" he asked the girl. She looked at Mr. Will with sad eyes and said, "I'm sorry, Mr. Will. I didn't know they were yours. Momma asked Daddy several months ago if that box was his and he said it was. I am so surprised at Daddy! I wonder why in the world he thought he could take your tools, and no one would know about it?" she said.

"Mr. Will, I would like to share something with you," she continued. "Did you know my dad when he was a young boy? The reason I'm asking, my mom told us all the things those people were saying about Dad at the funeral wasn't true. She said when Dad was a young boy, he had a bad habit of stealing. She said he went to prison one time. Have you ever heard this story?" she asked.

Mr. Will looked down at the floor while the girl spoke. "Yes. I heard about him going to prison and the reason why he went," said Mr. Will. "But that was when he was a teenager. We all have done wrong when we were young. I stole a lot of things in my youth, but I didn't get caught. That's the only difference between your dad and me. Don't hold that against your dad. When he died, he paid for all his wrong doings. If you girls live long enough, you too, will do something wrong. But remember, you must repent for your sins. No one can forgive you of your sins but God. Neither your mom nor your dad can go to God for you. You girls seem to be nice girls—stay that way. Let this be a lesson for you. Don't put yourself out there, then, people can't talk bad about you when you're dead and you can't defend yourself. Did you know, your name will go farther than any airplane will ever take you? I think I have said enough! I'll take those tools now! You girls have a nice day!" said Mr. Will.

Mr. Will drove home. Mrs. Olivia was sitting at the kitchen table when she saw Mr. Will pull into the yard. She got up to open the door for him. "Oh my goodness, he got his toolbox! I wonder what happened," she thought. As he walked in the house, she gave him a hug and asked, "Where did you find your tools?"

Mr. Will replied, "You know what, Honey? Every time I read my Bible, it's like the Lord is looking in my face as I read! I just read this morning about putting all your trust in people. Therefore, the Lord wants us to trust him and no one else. Man will deceive you and some of these women folks are worst. You know that boy had my tools in his closet! I was shocked when that child took me in his room. He had my tools sitting on the floor as if they were his. If he were here, I don't know what I would do to him! That thing made me mad! I have given him money and food out of my garden for helping me. He didn't have to steal from me. And the thought of me standing in the church in front of all those people, talking about how nice and good he was to everyone. If it would do any good, I would go to that graveyard and give him a piece of my mind!"

Mrs. Olivia watched as Mr. Will scolded Robert and acted as if he never knew what a Bible was. "Pa, don't talk like that! The boy is gone, now let him rest. He didn't know any better. Their mother had a hard time raising them. She didn't have a husband to help with those boys. They did good coming up as children. They didn't learn too much about life growing up, so don't talk about him. Let it go. God has blessed you to have more than enough. You just get yourself all worked up for nothing," she said as she continued her work.

Mr. Will finally calmed down. He took his collard plants outside. He counted them before putting them on the table. There were enough plants to fill his small garden area. Snow was standing near the garden. Every step Mr. Will made, Snow made one too. "Snow, don't you get in my garden. I don't want you near my collard plants. You stay away, you hear me," he told Snow. The dog walked away and sat down near the doorsteps. Mrs. Olivia watched them both through the kitchen window.

After preparing their dinner for the evening, she decided to read her Bible. Studying the Word always calmed her. "But when you ask, you must believe and not doubt, because the one who doubts is like a wave of the sea, blown and tossed by the wind. That person should not expect to receive anything from the Lord," she read from the book of James. "I wonder, did Pa pray over his garden spot before planting those collards? Now-a-day, you got to pray for everything you do, even planting food. He's putting a lot of money in the ground. He's got to put it in God's hand and watch God do His work. Believe and receive it. I always trust my God for everything I do," she said to herself with a heart of thanksgiving.

Mr. Will finished planting his garden. He gathered all his tools, went in the house for a bath and changed his clothes.

Now, he was ready for dinner and his favorite T.V. programs. "You know Honey, I was standing outside looking around and thinking to myself. Why are some of the limbs falling from my apple tree?" Mr. Will asked. "The tree is green in some places and looks as if it's dying in others. Paul talks about dying daily in the Bible. I got to do some research on that. Trees remind me of people—we are dying every day, and babies are born every hour. God knows what to do for His children. I believe that tree is me! There's a strange feeling I get when I'm near it. I feel like something is draining my insides. You understand what I'm saying! I can't explain it in words. There's something happening to me inside my soul. I feel a sadness and then I feel happy, all of this at the same time. Maybe, I need to ask the Lord to show it to me. What do you think?" he asked his wife, as he sat at the table for dinner.

"I think you are having a mid-life crisis!" she answered. "You're talking like my husband, but then, you're thinking like someone who I don't know.

You have done too much this week, Pa. Let your brain rest for a while. Your body is like a machine—you can't run it every day without letting it rest and putting fuel in it. I just hope you don't run yourself sick," she said, while folding her laundry.

Mr. Will gave her a puzzled look. He got up to get his Bible. He opened it to the Book of Psalms. As he turned the pages to chapter 1, he read out loud, "Blessed is the one who does not walk in step with the wicked or stand in the way that sinners take or sit in the company of mockers, but whose delight is in the law of the Lord, and who meditates on his law day and night. That person is like a tree planted by streams of water, which yields its fruit in season and whose leaf does not wither; whatever they do prospers."

He closed the Bible and looked at Mrs. Olivia. "Honey, you know something, I'm God's child and I feel as though I'm a blessed man. When I was young, I did some stupid things to other people, especially to the women. I know the things I did was stupid and wicked, but I have been forgiven for all that stuff. I don't have a desire to live like that now. I want to please the Lord for the rest of my life. Just think about that tree the Lord is talking about. I want to be like that. I want to be into the Lord so much that nothing will come in my life to make me turn around. A man is a fool to go to God, he saves him, and then he goes back to doing evil deeds again," said Mr. Will.

"You know, I have an idea!" said Mr. Will. "I'm going to save some of the seeds from my apple tree, let them dry out and put them in a bag for safe keeping. When the time is right, I'm going to give them to all my children. I want them to plant a seed in memory of me. I want all my children to pass it on to their children, and then their children. So, in other words, that tree will never die. When I am planted, I will live on and on through my children, my grandchildren, my great-grandchildren, and so on and so on. You understand?" he asked his wife.

Mrs. Olivia looked at him and nodded. She put her clothes away and prepared herself for bed. She knelt down beside her bed and prayed, *"Lord, you know all about that man of mine. Please give him understanding of Your Word. He's a good man and I love him so much. I don't know what's going on in his head. He will start one thing and then go back and do something else. He has come a long way, Lord. Keep him from all evil and don't let him falter. He loves his children and friends. He needs to let you do your planning for him and the children. We can't do nothing without You, Lord. Take care and guide him to do what is right. In Your Name I pray, Amen."*

CHAPTER 10

The Next Day

Breakfast was ready and it was Bible study time. Mrs. Olivia got her Bible and turned to the Book of Jeremiah. "Pa, you want to read this?" she asked as she handed the Bible to him. "What is it, Honey?" he asked, reaching for the Bible. He read, "The Lord came to me saying, 'What do you see, Jeremiah?' And I said, 'I see a rod of an almond tree.'" He added, "The Lord keeps talking to his children about trees. It happened years and years ago—from the beginning of time. The same way he talked to people back then, I think the Lord is talking to me too."

Mr. Will searched his Bible for more tree subjects. He read Psalm 52:8 about a green olive tree. Abram moved his tent by the oak tree and built an altar to the Lord. The Lord gave David instructions on how to defeat the Philistines using the balsam tree. The cedar tree, the fir, the cypress and the oak tree, were all in the Old Testament.

Mr. Will closed his Bible, and said to his wife, "Honey, I want to call a family meeting. I want all the children to come home one weekend. You call them and let them know. I got to do this before the Lord calls me home." Mrs. Olivia looked surprised. She put her dish towel down and sat in the chair next to her husband. "Pa, you not going anywhere no time soon. You have been a good father and husband for a long time. The Lord isn't going to take you like you think. He might be showing you how to spread His Word like we all should be doing. These children don't have time to come down here. They work five and six days a week, even on the weekend. They want to spend time with their family. Just plant your collard plants and save your apple seeds. Our family is going to prosper and grow with or without a tree," she said, as she rubbed on his arm.

Mr. Will seemed sad. "I don't want to be an old man who's always trying to find something to do, but if God is bugging me to do something, I think I should do it. Baby, you got to understand that I am a man. All my friends have gone on to be with the Lord. There's not much for an old man like me to do every day. You have your housework to do. You keep yourself busy going to the nursing home and going to your friend's homes to visit. I feel as though God is speaking directly to me. He talks to all His children. What he tells me, he may not tell you. Do you understand what I'm saying? Let me do what God wants me to do, and you do what God wants you to do. I love you, Baby! I love all my children. I want to make sure they all understand what I expect out of them when I'm gone. That tree is going to be there when we are long gone. If they cut it down, make sure they save and replant the seeds. I don't care where they plant them, just plant the seeds so my family will continue to be a part of me. I'm going to live forever through my children," said Mr. Will.

Mrs. Olivia looked at Mr. Will with tears in her eyes. She leaned over, kissed him on his head, and said, "You do what God wants you to do, and I'm sorry for questioning you about our God. I'm going to help you. I'll call the children tonight and see what they think about all of this."

Later that Evening

Mr. Will watered his collard plants. He gazed at his apple tree and said to himself, "It sure looks as if it's dead. The limbs are falling. Maybe I need to get someone to trim it. All trees turn dark in the fall and winter, but my tree has never looked this bad." He heard someone call his name. He turned around. It was Mr. Tee. "Hey man, what you know good?" Mr. Will asked. "Nothing at all, my friend. What are you doing?" asked Mr. Tee. "I was watering my collard plants and then I looked at this apple tree. It looks like it's dying. I know it turns dark in the winter, but never this dark. You know anything about trees?" he asked Mr. Tee. "Well, when I was a boy, my daddy had an apple tree in our back yard. There was an old man who lived down the road from us, who told daddy to put some fertilizer on it every other year. An apple tree does not produce every year, they take a break for a year, and when they do produce, you can pick up enough apples to feed an army. They will be plentiful! You'll have apples coming out your eyeballs," he said, smiling.

"You know what, man? You might have something there! I'll try that! I got to go to the hardware store tomorrow and I'll get me a bag. It's true; two heads are better than one!" said Mr. Will. They said their goodbyes and Mr. Will went into the house for the rest of the evening.

The Next Day

When 6 a.m. rolled around, there was fresh coffee in the pot, hot breakfast on the table and God's Word to read while Mr. Will ate breakfast. Mrs. Olivia always read a Bible verse to Mr. Will. Reading the Word always sounded better if she read to him.

He looked at his wife and said, "Honey, you know, I had the strangest dream last night. I dreamed about my momma and daddy. It was so real. I dreamed that I was a little baby boy. I had to be about a year old. I was sitting in Momma's lap and she was rubbing my hair. She was blessing me with her words. 'My little boy is so pretty,' she said. 'You are going to be a beautiful, bright, strong and prosperous man someday. You will have many children and more grandchildren than children, and so on. I will not see them all, but you will live a long life and you will enjoy them,'" he said while gazing at Mrs. Olivia. "I wonder why my momma came to me in my dream. I haven't thought about Momma and Daddy in a long time. Is there a sign for that, Honey?" he asked. Mrs. Olivia looked at him and said, "Maybe it's going to rain. Old folks say it's going to rain if you dream about the dead. Every time I have a dream like that, it rains!"

Mr. Will was puzzled. He got up from the table, grabbed his hat, and went outside. There was a dark cloud in the sky. He looked up and thanked God for another day. "Well, it looks like rain again. God knows what we need on this hill!" he thought. "Maybe my collard plants will grow like weeds this week. We are going to have collards to give away soon. Lord, I know you don't mean for us to charge our neighbors for what you have given us, but I've put a lot of work in this little garden. I got to get at least a dollar a collard. If they can't afford a dollar, then I'll just give them one. It won't hurt to ask for what I want. Lord, forgive me if I'm wrong," he said, as he walked between the rows of his garden.

The phone rang. Mrs. Olivia answered it. "Pa, come here. There's a little boy on the phone. He said he wants to say hello to his granddaddy. Hurry, Pa before he hangs up," she said. Mr. Will rushed in the house. He grabbed the phone and sat down in the chair at the table. "Which one of the babies is it?" he asked. Mrs. Olivia shrugged her shoulders.

"Hello, Baby. Who is this? Hello! Hello! Honey, that is the little boy who called last year. He said, 'Hey Granddaddy.' It sounds like our other grandboys, but I don't know. That bothers me! I got a funny feeling about this kid. I feel like he is part of my soul. I know I'm not going crazy, but this child called me Granddaddy like he knows me," said Mr. Will.

Mrs. Olivia stood by his side and said calmly, "The Lord is showing you something. That might be a token of your dream. Your momma was holding you in your dream. You saw yourself as a baby. She talked about children in the dream. I got to go in prayer about this. The Lord will reveal it, just watch and see, Pa."

Mr. Will looked at Mrs. Olivia. His heart was heavy, because he loved all his children and his grands were special to him. He sat quietly and whispered a prayer, *"Lord, please show this child to us. Don't let anybody hurt us by using a child. I'm asking you, Lord. In your mighty name I pray. Amen."*

Mrs. Olivia went to the bedroom to get her phone book. She looked for her daughter's number to call her and tell her the news. She remembered several years ago, one of their daughters told her that she heard their brother had a baby, but she didn't believe it. "Pa, we are going to get to the root of all of this," said Mrs. Olivia. "I'm calling the other children and see what they know. Somebody's going to tell us something."

Mr. Will got up from the table. He wiped his eyes with his handkerchief and put on his hat. "If you need me, I'll be outside on the porch. This thing is worrying me," he said as he sat down in his chair. "Honey!" he yelled to his wife. "Do you know where that picture is of the child? I want to look at it again. You told me a few years ago that the baby looked like our son. I didn't think so back then, but I believe it now," he said.

Mrs. Olivia got her picture album out and searched for the picture. Not long afterwards, she found it. "I got it, Pa. Now, look at this child, good! He got our baby's nose, mouth and head. Somebody knows something about this child, and I'm going to get to the bottom of it," she said.

The Next Day

Then came a new day and new business for Mr. Will. As he walked in his garden, he sprayed his collards with bug spray. He walked around the house to see if the ground was free of fallen limbs from his apple tree. He stood beside the tree and started to cry. He was feeling sorry for himself. He was an old man now. He knew that he didn't have many years left on this earth. Plans for his departure had to be made and made soon. He pondered his heart and began to pray. *"Lord, I know I don't have 20, 40, or even 45, more years on this earth, but if that baby is mine, please let me live to see him. I have a deep feeling in my soul about this child. Please Lord, let me live long enough to see this child, because I know in my heart, he is mine. Amen Jesus. Amen Lord."*

Mrs. Olivia called her husband to come in for breakfast. Mr. Will did not want the usual, this morning. He was okay with his coffee and toast. "Pa, don't you get yourself all worked up about that child. The girls said they didn't know who that was, and people will do anything to older people these days. They think that someone is playing tricks on you. Everybody knows that you love children. All the kids in this neighborhood call you 'Granddaddy,' and you have told your little jealous grand babies that you're everybody's Granddaddy. So, it might be a trick of the devil," she told him as he drank his coffee. "I've never thought about it that way. I prayed about it and I'm going to leave it in the hands of God," said Mr. Will.

Mr. Will finished his coffee and headed to the hardware store. On his way, he saw one of his friends, Poky, who needed a ride. He had worked with Mr. Will for years. He would mow the grass and trim the weeds around the house. "Get in, man. Where you headed early this morning?"

Mr. Will asked Poky. The truck window was down, and Poky reached in and opened the door. "Hey man. Give me a cigarette. I'm going down here to see if I can get a job at the Wal-Mart. I've been trying to get on there for months now. They want me to come in today and take a test. I hope I get this job. I'm tired of going to California," said Poky. They both looked at each other and laughed so hard Mr. Will almost ran off the highway. "You know what my wife says about that. She said, 'Stay in California, because they will feed you and give you somewhere to sleep. They'll keep you a little while, then, they'll let you out.'" Poky looked at Mr. Will with tears in his eyes from laughing at his jokes. "Yes, Momma always made fun of me about California. I love Momma. Where is she?" he asked. The answer was always the same. She was at home taking care of the house.

After an hour, Mr. Will arrived back home. He watered his house plants and turned the T.V. on to watch his favorite show.

12 Noon

Mrs. Olivia asked Pa to get his Bible. It was time to read the Word and say the noon prayer. Mr. Will turned his Bible to Psalm 90, one of his favorite Psalms. He read the entire Psalm. Then, he looked at his wife and asked her to search the Bible for a scripture that would tell him about children. He wanted to know what God said about the blessing of children.

Mrs. Olivia looked at him and wondered what was going on in his mind. "Pa, you still thinking about that child who called here? You need to let that go and give it to the Lord. You will worry yourself sick," she said. Mr. Will bowed his head sadly and said, "I want to get to the bottom of this. I'm not going to rest until I do. I know my children when I hear them.

I believe the Lord has already worked it out. It's up to us now. I'm going to find this child if it's the last thing I do. I want to feel him. If I get my hands on him, I'll know for sure he's my grand baby," said Mr. Will.

Mrs. Olivia had laundry to do, but her husband needed her to listen to him. She never like to see him sad, because he was always busy and out doing things that he enjoyed.

Mrs. Olivia turned her Bible to the book of Mark and said, "Look here, Pa! In Mark the ninth chapter, 36th verse it says, 'And he took a child and put him in the midst of them, and taking him in his arms, he said to them, 'Whoever receives one such child in my name receives me, and whoever receives me, receives not me but him who sent me.' Does that sound like the scripture you're looking for?" Mr. Will looked at the ceiling and shook his head. "No." he said. "I'm looking for a special scripture that's talking direct to me from the Lord, do you understand what I'm saying?"

Mrs. Olivia searched the Psalms. "Listen to this one, Pa. It comes from the 127th Psalm. 'Children are a gift from the Lord; they are a reward from Him'," read Mrs. Olivia. Mr. Will smiled, clapped his hands and yelled, "That's it! That's the words I want to hear. Children are a gift. This child is a gift that hasn't been opened yet. He is my present from the Lord. I can almost see it! The future is taking place in my mind. Honey, it's going to happen, you just wait and see. I'm going to leave it to the Good Master, he's going to work it out. Now, I can rest. That burden has lifted from my heart. I feel good now."

"Lord, I thank you," prayed Mr. Will. *"I thank you for what you are about to do in this family. I haven't seen this child yet, but I will before I leave this world."*

Mr. Will stood and began to sing "The Lord's Prayer." He sung himself happy. He wiped his eyes as he ended his solo. Mrs. Olivia screamed, "Hallelujah! Thank you Lord!" They praised the Lord so loud, that their neighbor, Mr. Tee, heard them and came over to see what was going on. When he knocked on the door, Mrs. Olivia opened it and grabbed his hand. "Thank the Lord, Brother Tee. The Spirit is in the house. We got to praise him in and out of seasons. Praise him when you're sick and when you're well. Praise him getting up and going down," said Mrs. Olivia.

Mr. Tee was in shock. He didn't know what to do or where to go. He started back out the door, but Mrs. Olivia had a grip on his arm and wouldn't let go. He looked at Mr. Will and saw that he was crying, so he started crying too. He didn't know why he was crying, but he felt happy inside. He was praising the Lord because he felt the Spirit come through Mrs. Olivia.

He walked over to the kitchen table where Mr. Will was sitting. "Sit down, Tee!" said Mr. Will. "Man, I feel good! I have another grandson somewhere. The Lord gave me this child as a gift, and he is going to be one of the best gifts from God above. I can feel it, Tee! When my wife read that scripture, Psalm 127 and said the 'reward' word, that was it!" said Mr. Will. "You know we have 10 children, and I know I'm going to have a lot of grands. I have six already, and just think, ten children having children. Man, the Lord is going to bless us with more grands than an apple tree can produce apples. I can see it, Tee. That's why I'm so happy," said Mr. Will.

Mr. Tee rested his arms on the table and asked Mr. Will, "How'd you find out about this child? You know people will fool you about these babies. All some of these girls want is a dollar. You better be careful, Will." Mr. Will looked at Mr. Tee and smiled. He said "This child called me, man! He called and asked for his granddaddy. He wanted to speak to me. I did hear somebody in the background, but the Lord is in this. Man, I haven't been a good person, but I believe in the Lord. The Lord loves me so much,

He's not going to allow some woman to make a fool out of me. I know what you mean, and a lot of people have been fooled to death, but not me! God is in this thing!" insisted Mr. Will.

Mr. Tee got up from the table and shook Mr. Will's hand, and said, "I'm proud for you, Will. If you believe that is your grandson, I believe it too. We didn't have but two children and I don't know what they gone do in life. If I get some grands, it will be fine, and if I don't, that will be fine too," said Mr. Tee.

The two men hugged and walked outside together.

CHAPTER 11

A Month Later

The collard plants had grown to be big bunches now. People were coming from miles away to buy Mr. Will's collards. He sold them for $1 a bunch. Mrs. Olivia collected the money and Mr. Will bagged the collards. "Pa, you made over $20 today. How many collards do you have left? You know the children want a bunch. You need to cut two for the holiday," she told Mr. Will. He walked in the house and got a bag. He cut the collards and Mrs. Olivia prepared them for her daughter.

As they were getting ready for dinner, a warning came on the T.V. concerning the weather. The news channel predicted a bad storm was heading their way. Mr. Will was terrified of storms. He would turn off all the electricity in the house when he heard thunder. "Close the curtains, Honey! Where can we hide? I hope the lights don't go out," he said as he tried to get close to Mrs. Olivia. She smiled at Mr. Will, and said, "Pa, you can't hide from the Lord. If he wants you, He's going to get you, no matter where you are. So, stop running and be still while the Lord is doing His work."

Mr. Will was stiff with fear. He sat close to his wife and didn't move. "I remember when I was a little girl, my Pa would hide in the closet and my Ma would laugh at him. She told Pa that the Lord knows where he is all the time, not just in the storm. My Pa would put dark quilts over the windows and wouldn't take them off until the storm was over. He didn't want us to move. We weren't allowed to talk, and we better not laugh and play during the storm. He made us read the Bible and pray—that's how I learned to read the Bible like I do. I would be so glad when the last thunder was heard. Old people would count the minutes between the first and last thunder, and they would be right too! When the last thunder was heard, Pa would take the quilts off the windows and open the door. We were so glad to get some air. I don't know why you so afraid of storms! You always lived in town. We were in the country—nothing but trees and sand," she said, as she sat with the Bible in her lap.

Mr. Will fell asleep in his chair. He didn't hear a word Mrs. Olivia said. He raised his head and looked around the room. "Is the storm over?" he asked Mrs. Olivia. She looked at him and smiled. "Yes, Pa. Take those quilts off the windows and open the door. I like to look out and see the damage from the storm. Do you want to eat now, or do you want to eat later?" she asked.

Mr. Will got up and sat at the table and asked for his coffee. "You know what Honey? The storm scared me so bad, I lost my appetite," said Mr. Will. "I don't need to eat this late. Put me a plate in the refrigerator for to-morrow. I got to get up early in the morning and cut some more collards. The season will be over soon. The Lord has been good to us this fall. We had apples and made pies, now the collard season is here. I think I'll go in the country tomorrow and get some salad greens. My friend Bill has a big patch in his back yard. If I pick it, he will give them to me. Do I have any doctor appointments this month?" he asked.

The Next Month

It was time for Mr. Will's annual check-up. He and Mrs. Olivia woke up early to get a fresh start. He couldn't eat this morning because he had to fast. He didn't like going to the doctors because he had to take off his clothes. His wife would be in the examining room with him, but that didn't matter. Taking off his clothes in front of a woman was uncomfortable to him. It didn't matter if Mrs. Olivia was in the room or not.

They were headed to Monroe. It was cold outside, and the news reported a possibility of snow was on the way. They arrived at 10 a.m. Mr. Will finished all his tests and could finally go and get something to eat. He loved the Chicken Box, so they ordered the usual: two-piece fried chicken with french fries, cole slaw and a biscuit.

Now, they were on their way back home. Mr. Will complained of having pains in his stomach. "I don't feel right in my stomach, Honey. The pain is getting worse as we get closer to home," he said. Mrs. Olivia glanced over her shoulder at him and asked why he didn't say something earlier. Mr. Will couldn't be still in his seat. He tried to move up and down in the car. He drunk a sip of water, but the pain got worse. "Do you want me to turn around and go back to the doctors?" asked Mrs Olivia. "You might have a blockage in your stomach, Pa. What do you want me to do? I can't read your mind," she said. Mr. Will didn't say a word. The expression on his face answered for him. Mrs. Olivia decided to take him to the ER in town. The doctors examined Mr. Will again and X-rayed his stomach.

One Hour Later

The results were back. Mr. Will had colon cancer. They were not happy about the news. When they arrived home, Mrs. Olivia called the children. Everyone was surprised. The doctors told Mr. Will that he was lucky. They caught the cancer just in time. The hospital scheduled Mr. Will to go in for surgery.

The Next Day

The surgery was scheduled for 7 a.m. All the children came home. When Mr. Will arrived at the hospital, the doctors asked who was there for emotional support for their mother. All the children raised their hands. Mrs. Olivia was in prayer for her husband as always.

One Hour Later

The surgery was a success. The doctors explained what to do to keep Mr. Will's body healthy. He had to change his diet. He could have no more fried foods, no hot sauce or other spicy foods. He had to drink more water. No smoking and drinking. He looked at the doctor and then looked at his children. "Dad, do you understand what the doctor is saying? You can't eat the way you used too. You can live a long healthy life if you listen to the doctors. We love you Daddy, and we want you to live a long time. You know, there are more grandchildren coming! We want you to be here to see them," his daughter explained to him. He smiled as she spoke. "I will, Baby. Your momma will see to that," said Mr. Will.

Three Days Later

Mrs. Olivia got up early and prepared breakfast. "How do you feel today, Pa?" she asked while stirring his coffee and filling his plate with food. Mr. Will smiled and said, "I feel better today than I've felt in a long time." He heard a sound outside. "Is that a car in the driveway? It looks like a woman's head in the driver's seat. It is! That's Ms. Richardson! Go to the door Baby, and let her in," said Mr. Will.

It was their friend from years ago. Ms. Richardson stepped up on the porch and greeted them while opening the door. "I'm coming in. Hello there!" she yelled. Mr. Will got up and gave her a big hug. Mrs. Olivia pulled a chair from the table and invited her to have a seat as the two greeted each other with a hug and a kiss on the cheek. "It's been a long-time, girl. You look so good! I see that life has treated you well, and God is still on his throne," said Mr. Will. "Ms. Richardson has always been a beautiful woman. Her mom and daddy were beautiful people. All of you have that smile. I can tell you Richardsons from anybody else in town. You all got a piece of gold in the front of your mouth and have pretty-curly hair. The Lord knew what he was doing when He picked your mom for your daddy," said Mr. Will.

Mrs. Olivia asked, "How many children were in your family?" Ms. Richardson smiled and answered, "There were ten of us, and only three of us are living. The Lord has really been good to me and my family. My daddy worked on the farm and all his children went to college except me and some of the boys. I went to trade school. I was slow to learn in school. My sisters were very smart, but all I wanted to do was followed my daddy around the farm. He taught me how to plow the mule and milk the cows. I remember when he taught me how to shoot his shot gun. I could hit a snake within 50 feet from where I stood. I was just that good!" she said.

"You know, Ms. Richardson, I will never forget your family. Your sister was an amazing woman. I worked at the old White school for many years. I had to raise my children on $125 a month. If it hadn't been for the good Lord and your sister, I don't know what would have happened to me and my family. Men like me cared about the welfare of our families. My wife cooked three times a day. My children ate good every day. My chil-dren went to the store and got food on credit if they didn't want what she cooked. Ms. Robinson would let them have anything they wanted. Ms. Cora would give them a ten cents ice cream cone for five cents. Some of my children would tell you today; they never went hungry. It brings tears to my eyes just thinking about how hard it was for me and my wife. Every pay day, I made sure that your sister had her money. I had to pay the light bill, water bill, house rent, car insurance, buy clothes for my children and buy food out of $125 a month. I can't believe how the Lord made a way for me back then. Nobody knows my story, but God," cried Mr. Will.

Ms. Richardson looked at Mr. Will's teary eyes and said, "It was God! We all had a rough time back then. The only difference was, we were a little more advanced than most people. We owned a farm. My dad grew most of everything we ate. We had mules, cows, chickens, goats, ducks, hogs and pigs. The only thing we bought from town was sugar, flour, meal and coffee. Just be thankful that God showed favor for your family. He's a God that never fails. He's slow to anger and he loves all of us. Now, I'm going to get to the main reason I stopped by here! I heard you have an apple tree in your back yard."

Mr. Will got up from the table and asked Mrs. Olivia for a bag. He said to Ms. Richardson, "Come on girl. Let's go down here! I got some apples in my freezer. You can have some of these. My tree didn't produce that well this year, but next season, I'm looking for this yard to be covered. I don't know what you're going to make, but these are good for pies and dumplings," Mr. Will said, as he handed her the bag.

"Didn't come to be greedy. I only wanted a few for a pie," said Ms. Richardson. "I thank you so much. Since my sister moved away, I don't cook like I did when she was home. I won't go back up those steps. Tell your wife I said good-bye. I will come by again so we can continue our conversation about the old ole days," she said, as she opened the back door and walked to her car. Mr. Will followed her outside and waved goodbye.

As he walked on the front porch, he sat down in his rocking chair and bowed his head in a silent prayer. Mrs. Olivia watched. She thought he was asleep, but she knew what was going on. She loved her husband and always watched his every move. She knew that his health wasn't like it was when he was young and things were going to get worse. She opened the front door and asked, "Pa, are you sleep?" Mr. Will opened one eye and looked back at the door, "Um, nope. I just closed my eyes for a minute." Mrs. Olivia stepped out the door and said, "Come on in before these bees sting you. You're sitting out here without your hat, and the bees are flying around your bald head. Get up! Come in the house!" He got up and walked inside. Mrs. Olivia helped him to the bedroom so he could take a nap.

CHAPTER 12

Early the Next Morning

There was an EMS truck at Mr. Tee's house. Mrs. Olivia could see it from their kitchen window. "Pa!" she yelled. "Come here. I believe something is wrong with Tee or his wife." Mr. Will hurried to the kitchen. He looked out the window and saw the EMS truck in their driveway. "I wonder who they called them for! Tee didn't seem to be sick the other day, and he said his wife was doing fine. Let me go outside and see what they are doing" he said, as he walked out the side door.

When he got outside, he saw the paramedics carry what looked like Tee on a stretcher. He walked to the road near Tee's house. He saw Tee's wife. "Is everything okay over here?" he asked the wife. "No, Will. Tee just had a stroke," his wife said. "I had to call 911 this morning. I'm going to the hospital with the EMS. I'll come out there when I get back. Would you please watch my house for me? Tell your wife to watch for my daughter when she comes, and let her know what happened, and where I am." Mr. Will walked back to the house. He told Mrs. Olivia what Tee's wife said. "I hope he will be alright. Things can happen so fast. You're up today and gone tomorrow," he said as he walked in the house for breakfast.

That Afternoon

The cars owned by the family had filled the driveway and in front of Mr. Tee's house. His wife walked over to Mr. Will and Mrs. Olivia. Mr. Will saw her coming and met her at the door. As she walked in, Mr. Will could see how sad she looked. "It doesn't look good," she said. "Tee had a bad stroke to his brain. The doctors said he will never come back home. The children and I must decide where to put him. I just don't know what to do. This is my first time ever having something like this to happen to us. Mrs. Olivia, you helped at one of the rest homes here. What do you think?" she asked, crying. Mrs. Olivia asked her to sit down. She told her that the rest home in town would be the best place for Mr. Tee. She and Mr. Will offered to help in any way that they could. "Tee has always been a good neighbor to us. I hate that this happened. I knew he had high blood pressure, but I didn't know it was that bad. You go on home with your children. If you need me for anything, just let us know. I love that man. We will be in prayer for you both," Mr. Will said as they walked her outside.

One Week Later

The news was all over town. Mr. Tee died. It was sad that Mr. Will had to hear the news while out shopping for grocery. One of his friends from work saw him in the store and told him about Tee. He was shocked to know that another one of his friends had passed away. He got in his truck and drove home.

As he removed the groceries from his truck, Mrs. Olivia was watching from the living room window. She walked outside to help Mr. Will. As she got closer to him, she noticed that he was crying. "What's wrong with you, Pa?" He turned and said, "Tee died today. One of the guys saw me at the store and told me. I wanted to go see him this week, but now, I don't have to go. He's gone to be with the Lord," he said. Mrs. Olivia took one of the bags from him, closed the truck door, and said, "He's better off, Pa. He's not suffering anymore. No more pain. No more buying medicine. No more going to the doctors. The Lord knows best for us all."

One Afternoon

Mr. Will awoke from his afternoon nap. He walked to the back yard where his apple tree was. He noticed that another limb had fallen off the tree. He picked up the limb and thought "I wonder why this limb broke off my tree. It seemed to be a healthy limb! It's color inside is fresh looking and the wood feels smooth and healthy. It just fell off for no reason, or did it fall for a reason? It seems to me, every time one of my friends pass away, I lose one of my limbs from this tree. Robert was the first one, now Tee!" He threw the limb across the street into the woods.

Mr. Will looked at the tree. A strange feeling came over him. It seemed that the tree was drawing him close to its trunk. It was like electricity! Mr. Will started sweating and reaching for the tree at the same time. He tried to pull away from the tree, but the tree had a force like no other. All at once, his hands locked around the tree. He couldn't control himself. There was a burning feeling from the tree. Mr. Will let go. "Oh, Lord! What happened to me? Something has left my body!" He looked down at his knees, and they were shaking and knocking together. Water was pouring down his face. He looked at his hands and they were shaking. "Did I have a stroke? Maybe I had a heart attack! Whatever that was, I feel good inside. God has changed me from the inside out. I can't tell anybody about this. They will think I'm losing my mind," he thought, as he examined himself and walked to the house. Mrs. Olivia was sitting at the table. "Pa, you're wet. You look pale in the face. Are you alright?" she asked. Mr. Will kept silent. He sat down in his chair and smiled.

Later that Evening

Mr. Will wanted to know when and where Tee's funeral was going to be. He walked across the street and asked Tee's wife for information. The funeral would be held at Tee's home church outside of town. The family was planning to lay him to rest in the family plot at the church on Friday at 2 p.m.

Friday, Going Home Service for Mr. Tee

Everyone in town knew that Mr. Will and Tee were good friends. Once again, Mr. Will was asked to make remarks and sing "The Lord's Prayer." He had talked about going to the funeral with his wife, but he didn't want to sing. He wanted to make remarks and let that be. "I really don't want to go today. Going to funerals makes me feel so down-hearted and sad," he said. "Those children crying for their dad and his wife trying to console them...it just gets next to me. But he was my friend and the least I can do is to go and say something," said Mr. Will.

Later that Afternoon

Mr. Will and his wife arrived at 1 p.m. When the service began at 1:45 p.m., the pastor invited Mr. Will to come to the podium. Mr. Will did a beautiful opening of the service. He asked everyone except the family to stand in honor of the long life of his friend, Tee. He spoke with clarity. He spoke with love for the family. And right before he finished his speech, he sang "The Lord's Prayer."

When he opened his mouth, everyone was in awe! Mr. Will sang better than he had ever sung before. He took the microphone from the podium. He walked all over the church. He raised his hands to the Lord. People were standing up and yelling, "Sing that song, Will!" They stood and clapped for Mr. Will for several minutes. The Holy Spirit had taken over. He ended the song while walking back to his seat to be with his wife. The funeral lasted for about an hour. Mr. Tee was laid to rest and everyone went home.

"It's going to be lonesome on this hill. I think I'm the only old man over here now," he said to his wife. She looked at him and said, "No, you're not, Pa. You still got Mr. Edward, Mr. Parker, Mr. Bill, your brothers and Chavis. Enjoy yourself and your friends. You don't know when the Lord is coming back for us. It will be warm soon. You can get back into your apple pie making business. The tree is going to have a lot of apples this year," she said. Mr. Will looked at her and smiled.

CHAPTER 13

The Next Month

All day long, rain was falling. The clouds were gray. Mr. Will didn't have anything to do. The phone rang. Mrs. Olivia answered.

"Pa, it's the little boy again. He wants to talk to Granddaddy. Hurry to the phone." Mr. Will got up and took the phone, and said, "Hello! Who am I talking to? Baby, what is your name and who is your mother?" Mrs. Olivia looked surprised. She waited until Mr. Will got an answer. "Who did you say?" asked Mr. Will. Then, the child hung up. Mr. Will sat down and wiped his head with his handkerchief. "I don't know why people do stuff like this. Why would they worry me? Maybe he will call back later," Mr. Will said as he hung up the phone.

As soon as he sat down, the phone rang again! He got up to answer the phone a second time. "Hello, hello. I said, hello," said Mr. Will. In that same moment, a young boy yelled, "Hello, Granddaddy! My name is Dennis. I love you and Grandma. Can you hear me Granddaddy? This is Dennis!" Mr. Will called his wife to come listen. "Dennis, who? Who are you, son and who are you calling for? We don't have a grandchild named Dennis. Is there anyone else at home with you? I want to speak to your mother." There was no response. The young child on the other end of the phone hung up. Mrs. Olivia was speechless. She helped Mr. Will to the sofa. He wiped his eyes with his handkerchief.

"This is really getting to me. This child sounds just like our other grandchildren. I'm going to make some phone calls. Somebody knows something about this child. He's our grand baby! I can feel it in my soul. The Lord is going to fix it so it will be told to us. I'm just that crazy to believe everything about my God. He never makes a mistake. Everything done in the dark will come to light. I believe he is going to fix everything. You just watch and see, Honey," he said, as he held Mrs. Olivia's hand.

CHAPTER 14

Months Later

The weather was changing, and the season was over for collards. Mr. Will was getting ready for apple season again. This year was the year of Jubilee. The harvest would be plentiful. The apple tree was full of young apples. Mr. Will was up early this morning. He ate breakfast at the usual time and said the morning prayer. Mrs. Olivia was washing her laundry and cleaning the house. It was 8 a.m.

The phone rang in the kitchen. "Pa, somebody wants to talk to you. It sounds like your friend who you worked with. Hurry, Pa," said Mrs. Olivia. Mr. Will dropped everything and rushed to the phone. "Hello, Will speaking," said Mr. Will. "You found out WHAT? I'll be down there in a few minutes," he told his friend.

Mr. Will prepared to go see his friend. He told his wife that he would be back soon, and he would tell her the news when he got back. Mrs. Olivia got his keys and hat, then walked him to the door.

One Hour Later

When Mr. Will pulled up in the driveway, Mrs. Olivia was standing in the doorway waiting for the news. "Honey, you got to sit down. I got the best news of our life," said Mr. Will. "You know that baby who was calling here? Well, his grandmother works with my friend," said Mr. Will. "They didn't know each other on their job, but one day while on their lunch break, they started a conversation. She told her that her daughter had a baby by a young man who lives in this neighborhood. She called our son's name and said he was her grandchild's father. She gave my friend a picture of the child. He's a big boy now! I told you the Lord was going to work this thing out. I prayed about it and left it alone. My God never disappoints us. We disappoint him when we don't wait. Look at this fine boy!" he said while giving the picture to his wife. They were so happy about the good news.

Mrs. Olivia called everybody she knew. While sitting in her chair gazing at the child's picture, she thought about one more person, her son, the child's father. She called him on the phone and told him what happened. He told his mom that he couldn't believe it! Having another son who he didn't know about, was going to be a shock to his family. After Mrs. Olivia broke the news to her son, she called her oldest daughter. She wanted her to see the picture. As strange as it was, everyone in the family was excited about the new addition to the family.

Three Months Later

Little Dennis's mom called to let everyone know that she and the child would be coming home to North Carolina. The family was waiting for the grand surprise!

When Edward came by to see Mr. Will, he couldn't keep the news to himself. "Have a seat, man. I'm so excited, I don't know what to do," Mr. Will said, as Edward asked for something to drink. "What is it? Did you win some money, or did you win the lottery?" Edward asked. "No, man! I found out a few weeks ago that we have another grandchild, and he's coming the end of this week." Edward smiled widely and asked, "Which one of your children going to have another baby? I thought you told me that all your children were getting too old to have more children. You want great grands, now!" Mr. Will didn't know what to say. He paused for a moment until he could not hold it any longer.

"Well, I didn't share this with you, but for months now, this kid has been calling the house for me. He always called me 'Granddaddy.' He sounded just like my other grands, but I didn't know who it was. It bothered me for a long time, and I prayed about. I wanted God to show this child to us if he was ours, and he did. The good news is, it's true. God has answered my prayer," said Mr. Will, with his heart full of gratitude. He was so grateful for all the blessings God had granted to him and his family.

He took his handkerchief out his pocket and wiped his eyes and said, "You know man, I consider you as being one of my closest friends. We went to war at the same time. I was a young man when I got married. I had my first son when I was 25 years old. I didn't know how to be a father. I thought raising a child was the way my daddy raised me. I didn't like the way I was raised, but when I look back over my life, my daddy did the best of what he knew. My son was a good kid growing up, but I feel as though I failed him in so many ways. When he was going to school with all the black children, he did well in school. As soon as the county decided to build the new school for our children and mixed all the children together, something bad happened. We didn't have any problems with our children. One day my boy came home and told us that he was suspended from school for the year. I couldn't believe it. Everything at that new school was white. The principal, assistant principal, teachers and even the bus drivers were majority white," said Mr. Will.

"Those white people did what they wanted to do to our children. It was told to me that my son and two other boys left campus early and came back to school. They could do that because it was the end of the year and they were testing. All the children who didn't have to test could leave school and come back if they wanted to. When my boy and the other boys came back, the principal was standing in the door. He opened the door for them. As they walked in the building, he told them that he smelled alcohol on them. He suspended the boys at that moment. He told them to leave and never come back. All three boys left the school. They were afraid to go home and tell their parents what happened. That thing did something to me. I loved my son. I wanted my first child to graduate from high school like all the other children. It bothered me for a long time. But you know what? Those white people thought they were hurting our black children. He had to get a job and earn money the best way he could. He moved from this town and went to Charlotte. When I say God turned it around; he did more than just turn it around. My son is one of the most intelligent, smart, educated, prosperous black men a father could ever dream of. He had it hard for a while, but God blessed him to get a good job in Charlotte. He was an excellent employee for that company he worked for. They found out that he hadn't completed high school, so they sent him back to school to get his GED. After receiving his GED certificate, the instructors at the college encouraged him to go another two years and get his B.S. degree. He was excellent in Math! I was so proud of that young man. I cried when the children told me what he had done. I know he made a mistake in getting this child, but God turned that problem about school around and he is going to turn this mistake into a big blessing. I might not be here to see it, I'm just that crazy about God to believe it. You watch and see, my friend," Mr. Will said as he wiped his eyes.

Edward didn't know what to say. He reached in his pocket and got himself a plug of tobacco and said, "You know, we all had a rough time growing up. These children have it better than we did. I have so many sad stories inside of me, I believe I would go crazy if it weren't for the Lord on my side. At least, you and your children had a daddy. I didn't! It was just my mom and her children. You talk about rough! We had it! God is going to turn this thing around one day. Our children are going to make up for what we didn't have," said Edward.

"So, getting back to your grand boy, is your son coming home to see him too?" he asked Mr. Will. "Yes. He's coming because he didn't know about the kid. This young girl had the child and didn't want our family to know about him. My wife talked with her on the phone. She said it was her mistake and she was going to raise him without his father. She didn't want anything from my son, so she didn't tell him. It was the child who wanted to know who his father was. He also wanted to know if he had another Grandma and Granddaddy. She had to tell him sooner or later. But you know what? It seems bad, but God is going to get the glory out of this thing. Sometimes, we think we'll doing things on our own, but it's not our doings; it's God working behind the scene. If you don't believe it, just look at David in the Bible. Look what he did. God was all in it. God loves messy people. He can take a mess to show others what he can do. He uses us for His good!" said Mr. Will. "I can't wait to put my hands on that child. I want to look in his eyes and put a blessing on him. I feel it in my bones, man! God is going to surprise us all with this one. Just wait and see," he cried to his friend.

The next morning, Mr. Will got up early and walked to see his apple tree. He kneeled to the ground and said a prayer. As he began to pray, he noticed a new tiny limb growing on the side of the tree. It had fresh green leaves. *"God always give me a sign with this tree. He is showing me that someone new is coming and it's a part of my body. This child is going to be a part of this tree. He is my seed!"*

He prayed, *"Father God. I want to give you all the praise this morning for who you are. You made the sun and it obeyed your will. You made the moon to shine when darkness of time was present. You spoke and the wind and rain came to rescue us from the dry places in our lives. Everything obeys except man. I am a sinner, Lord. I ask you to forgive me of my sins. I thank you for this day and all my daily bread for my body. Bless my family, Lord. Bless my family in ways that will please you. Cover each one of us with your love and guidance. I need you to increase my faith. Increase my giving. Increase my forgiveness, so whatever I have done wrong to others it won't block my blessings. I know you have your eyes on my family. Don't ever leave us alone. Be with my friends and my enemies, for I have many. Keep Satan's hands off my family, my home, my finances, and my apple tree. I need you to keep blessing my property. And, if it is your will, Lord. I pray this prayer in your Holy name. Amen."*

Mr. Will gathered his tools from the barn. Snow walked behind him wagging his tail. "Snow, you know what? This is a mean old world we live in. But God is going to work everything out in His own time. I got a jewel here! My family is my jewel. A poor man like me, has created many gifts that the Lord is going to use for His glory. All my boys are fine young men. Decent, respectful black men, and the Lord is going to bless every one of them, you just watch and see, boy," he said while rubbing and loving on his dog.

Mrs. Olivia cleaned her house and did the regular chores for that morning. They decided to go out for dinner. Mr. Will always liked going to one of the fish restaurants in town. They were so happy, riding around town and enjoying themselves.

"Take me by Chavis's house for a minute, Baby. I need to tell him the good news," he told his wife. Mrs. Olivia turned her car around and drove to their friend's house. "I don't think he's home, Pa. He might be at the doctor. You know he has problems with his eyes. You get out and go to the door. If he's in there, don't go in and stay. You come on back so we can be home before dark." Mr. Will did as she said.

When he knocked on the door, Chavis opened the door and asked him to come in. But Mr. Will stood in the door and chatted with his friend. "Man, I got the best news ever. You know that child I was telling you about? Well, his momma is bringing him to the house so we can meet him. We are so happy about it. I told you the Lord was going to fix that thing, and he did," he explained.

The friends were thrilled about the new addition to the family. Chavis walked Mr. Will to his car. He greeted Mrs. Olivia and they said their good-byes. Mrs. Olivia drove home. She was happy to see her husband excited about the grandchild. It was a worry of his for months, and finally, the time had come to see the child that Mr. Will knew was his all along.

CHAPTER 15

The Following Weekend

Family members came from near and far to see the new addition. They all gathered at Mr. Will's home. When the little boy and his mother stepped on the porch, Mr. Will was the first one to open the door.

"Come on in. Oh my! How are you, young lady? And look at this fine young boy. Come here, baby. You look so much like your daddy," he said as he picked the child up in his arms. He rubbed the boy's head and looked him in the eyes. Mrs. Olivia came over to meet her new grand. "Look at his hands, Pa. They are the same shape as his daddy's. He has his dad's lips and head. Everything about him is just like his daddy. This is a blessing from the Lord. Nobody can do this but God," she cried as she and her husband enjoyed examining their new grand.

In the same hour, their son from Charlotte came to the door. He walked in the house and saw everyone gathered around the child. "Hey, hey! Hey Mom and Pops!" He looked at the young woman whom he hadn't seen in years. He gave her a hug and greeted her and the child.

"You don't have to say anything about the child. I didn't know, but that doesn't matter now," said their son. "He is here and we are going to love him with all we have. I want you to know that God was in this all the time. Everything worked out for the best. I'm just thankful that Mom and Dad are still here to see my baby. We want him to be happy and meet his other brother and sister. He has a multitude of first cousins on my side of the family. Please stay in touch with us so we can keep up with him. I want to know about his school and activities. If you need anything for him, please let me know. God will work everything out for His good," he said as he held his son in his arms.

Little Dennis and his mom said good-bye and left to go home. Mr. Will was so happy about their visit. "I'm telling you, that's a fine boy. When I held him in my arms, I knew he was mine. My heart felt good. The Lord don't lead me wrong. I can feel my own blood. All it takes is a feel. If I put my hands on any of these children, I can feel myself inside of them. These girl's children are automatically mine, but the boys, I don't know for sure until I see them. When that child called me for the first time, I felt it in my heart that he was ours. God is so good! I don't doubt Him, because I know too much about Him," he praised the Lord while talking to his son.

CHAPTER 16

Months Passed

The weather was getting warmer and Mr. Will kept busy in the yard. He mowed the lawn on Fridays. He washed his car on Saturdays. On Monday through Thursday, he would work in his garden or pick apples and peaches.

One of his neighborhood friends would come by and pick a shirt tail full of peaches every summer. His friend was also the neighborhood plumber. Anything Mr. Will needed fixing, this friend could do it. "Hey there, Will. What's going on with you? I see the tree is going to have a lot of peaches this year, and I'm going to get my fill of them. Did you hear what I said, Buddy?" asked his friend. Mr. Will smiled and said, "Man, if you come near my peaches before I get one, I'm going to give you the whipping your momma should have given you," laughed Mr. Will, as he reached for his friend's hand. "What's going on with you today? I haven't seen you in a while. I needed you last week to look at my outside faucet. I have a hard time turning it off and on. You don't have to look at it today, just when you have time. Have you heard about my new grand boy?" Mr. Will asked.

The young man looked at Mr. Will as if he didn't hear him clearly. "Well, somebody told me that you all had a time up here a few months ago," said his friend. They said the yard was full of cars. They asked me what was going on and I told them I didn't know. So that's what it was. Where did this new grand come from and who had him?" he asked.

Mr. Will paused for a second and said, "My oldest son. Well, I'm going to tell you like this; the Lord sent him to us. You know God can give gifts to His children. Don't you have some children?" Mr. Will's friend nodded, looking puzzled. "You thought your wife or the woman who had the baby gave it to you, but you're wrong. God gave you that child. God doesn't give women folks children, he gives the man the babies, the woman just carries the baby for him. Do you get what I'm saying?" asked Mr. Will.

"Yes. You got a point there. Will, I got to get on down the road. I started over across the highway to do some work for Edward. I'll be back one day next week to fix that faucet," said his friend. Mr. Will agreed and asked his friend how much was he going to charge him for his labor. The man responded, "You know how we do! A shirt full of peaches for a job well done." The two friends smiled at each other as they parted ways.

It was time for lunch. Mrs. Olivia answered the phone just as Mr. Will was walking in the door. "Pa, this is little Dennis' mom and she wants to bring him home for a 'Welcome to the Family' party. Here, come get the phone," she said, as she handed Mr. Will the phone. "Hello, darling. That will be fine. I'll let everyone know. You all be safe until we see you next week," he told the child's mom. Mr. Will was excited. He loved family gatherings. A party at his home was going to be great. He sat down at the table and ate his lunch.

He told Mrs. Olivia that he had to go to the bank and get some money. He wanted to get all the food so the only thing the children had to do was come home. "Honey, I want to get a roast, hot dogs, and ribs. And ask the Baby to make a big mac and cheese—enough to feed everybody. Do you think we need a tossed salad to go with the food? Oh yes, I need to get canned sodas and bottled water. We need to put them in the refrigerator so they will be cold. I got to get plates, forks, napkins and cups," said Mr. Will.

Mrs. Olivia looked at him in amazement. "Pa, you just going overboard with this party. You don't need to get all that food!" she said. "You don't know who's coming, yet. Wait and see what the Baby say. She will ask around and see who is coming and what everyone else want to bring. You want food that you like to eat. You got to remember, it's getting warm now, and people don't want all that meat. Hot Dogs and hamburgers will be enough. If the Baby wants to make mac & cheese and a salad, that will be enough," she said. "You're getting too excited. The children want to enjoy the child and not spend all their time eating," she said to her husband. Mr. Will thought about it and said, "You're right, Honey! When someone says 'party' to me, I want to have a party. I want everybody to come and have a good time," he added.

"Pa, don't you get too excited and bring out your little drink downstairs. You know how you get with that little drink. These children aren't coming to hear you talk all that liquor talk. They want to come see the child and go back home," said Mrs. Olivia. Mr. Will looked at Mrs. Olivia and said, "I know what I want to do. If I want a little wine to celebrate, I can have me some and give some to whoever want some!" said Mr. Will. "Baby, I love you. I think you are a good Christian too, but you don't understand your Bible. You read it every day and you miss some of the most important parts in it. Haven't you read where the Lord made wine for the bride and groom's wedding reception? They had wine and they drank it too. When they ran out, Jesus' mother told him that they were out of wine and He turned the water that was in the water jugs into wine. I didn't make this story up just to have wine for our party. It's true! God made the wine and I'm going to enjoy me some at my party, and that is that!" said Mr. Will.

Mrs. Olivia was silent. She never argued with her husband. Whenever he set his mind on what he wanted to do, that was the way it was going to be. She looked at him and smiled to herself. "When you go to the bank, get enough money to buy what you need and no more. It doesn't take all your check to feed these children. You need to call them and see who's coming. Some of them may have to work," she advised her husband.

The weather report on T.V. advised that a storm was coming through the county. Mr. Will walked outside to check on his apple tree. The wind was blowing and the trees were swaying back and forth. Trash was flying in his yard from the neighbor's house. He ran inside to get a trash bag. The rain poured down like water from an opened well. Mrs. Olivia walked outside to give him a coat to cover himself. "Pa, don't you fall! Put that coat over your head and back," she scolded her husband. Mr. Will did as she asked.

He walked around the house to his garden spot. He noticed that another large tree limb had fallen from the top of his apple tree. He picked up the limb and examined it. He wondered why a healthy limb like this just broke off for no reason. Tears rolled down his face. It was going to be bad news for him. He remembered that when the other limbs fell, he lost two of his best friends. He took the limb and placed it behind the house. As he walked away, he looked back at his tree and said a silent prayer.

Lord, here I am again. I know you don't mind your children calling on you. It's my tree again! Show me what it is! I'm leaving it in your hands, Amen! It was always a good idea to pray when something unusual happened.

He went inside and sat in his chair. He took a handkerchief out his pocket and wiped his face and eyes. "What's wrong, Pa? Is that rain or have you been crying?" Mr. Will shook his head. When he looked up at Mrs. Olivia, tears rolled down his face like drops of sweat. "You know, when I was outside during the storm, I checked on the garden spot and the apple tree. I saw a big limb on the ground. It fell from the top of my tree. That is a bad sign! I've noticed something. Every time one of the limbs fall, someone who is close to me passes away. But, this time, I feel different. It's really hurting my heart. I'm about to be sick over this one. I had to go in prayer. God is testing me, this time! That limb was so perfect! Nothing was wrong with it. I feel like it's my right arm missing. I'm telling you, Honey. There's a sadness that has taken over my spirit," he said.

Mrs. Olivia sat down beside her husband and rubbed his hand. "The Lord will show you what it is, Pa. Before you read your Bible tonight, ask the Lord to show you what he wants you to know about that tree. It worked before, and it will work again," she said, as she held her face close to his.

Later that Night

Mr. Will got his Bible. When he opened it, the pages seemed to open to the book of John. He started reading aloud. "Let not your heart be troubled; you believe in God, believe also in Me. In My Father's house are many mansions; if it were not so, I would have told you. I go to prepare a place for you. And if I go to prepare a place for you, I will come again and receive you to Myself; that where I am, there you may be also. And where I go you know, and the way you know."

He closed his eyes. Mrs. Olivia watched him for a moment. She thought he was asleep, but he sat up in his chair and started reading again. "Jesus answered and said to him, 'If anyone loves Me, he will keep My word; and My Father will love him, and We will come to him and make Our home with him.'"

Mr. Will raised his head and looked at his wife. "I feel better now. The Lord is going to move in this house. I don't know where it's going to happen, but it's going to happen. I'm finished with it! I'm not going to worry about it anymore. When God is on your side, why let what you can't do anything about keep us from enjoying ourselves?" he said as he closed his Bible and put it away.

CHAPTER 17

Morning prayer was said and Mr. Will was ready for his children. He prepared all the meat and had the grill clean and ready to light. Mrs. Olivia was on the phone with her daughter. She and Mr. Will had already cooked all the vegetables and had the condiments ready for the table. Three of the boys came early to help their dad cook the meat. The girls who lived out of town were on their way.

Mr. Will went outside to set the tables and chairs. As he was leaning over, he saw a car pull up in the yard that he didn't recognize. He stood there for a while and watched to see who was going to get out. It was Little Dennis and his mom! He stopped what he was doing and rushed to their car. "Hello there. You all come on in the house." As Little Dennis got out the car, Mr. Will grabbed him and gave him a big hug. "Son, you look so good! I'm glad to see you and your mom. Go on in the house. Your Grandma is waiting on you." Little Dennis and his mom went inside. Mrs. Olivia and the boys gathered around the boy and greeted them with hugs and kisses.

After about an hour, the girls arrived with the food. Everyone at the party stood and held hands to say the blessing. As they held hands, Mr. Will started talking and tears rolled down his face. "I'm sorry children. But I am so happy. I prayed to my Father in Heaven for this day, now it is here. God has been so good to me and my family. He has given me more seeds than I will ever be able to count. You all don't know what that means, but you will when your momma and I are gone on to Heaven," he said.

He turned to little Dennis. "Young man, God is going to bless you in ways you will never know. I may not be here in the flesh, but I will be here in the spirit. I can see it with my spiritual eyes. You all don't understand that talk; it's from God. Don't you all ever forget about the goodness of our Heavenly Father. He did it! Everything that has happened here, he did it! Don't forget what I'm saying. Go ahead, son, and bless the food," said Mr. Will. The blessing was said by the preacher in the family. Everyone who was present said something loving and encouraging to Little Dennis and his mother.

The Party Begins

Everyone was outside at the picnic tables. The music was playing loud enough for the neighbors on the other street to hear. People came from near and far. Mrs. Olivia called some of her close relatives to come get a plate of food.

The other grandchildren danced and entertained Little Dennis as if they knew him all their lives. They had games, baseballs, and bats. There were basketballs and hula hoops, jump ropes, and a small swimming pool for the babies. Everyone at the party had a great time. They ate all the hamburgers and hot dogs. Mrs. Olivia stood back and watch the food disappear from the table. She enjoyed seeing her children and grandchildren eat.

At the end of the party, all the men cleaned the yard and the women washed the dishes and pans. When the chores were finished, everyone gathered again to say a parting prayer. Mrs. Olivia said the prayer. When she prayed, she prayed with authority! She knew how to call on the Lord.

She anointed the ones who were ill or just wanted to be anointed by their mother. When she finished the prayer, everyone got in their cars and headed to their homes.

Hours Later

The house was quiet again. Mr. Will sat outside on his picnic table. One of the neighbors came by. "Mr. Will, I see that you all had a big crowd here today. Did all your children come home?" the young man asked. Mr. Will invited the man to have a seat near him. "Yes, and we had a good time today. I saw you across the street and thought you were coming over. When I have something over here, I want all my friends to come! You know how we do. We had so much food, we told the children to take some home with them."

The young man enjoyed Mr. Will's stories about his family. "I wish my family would get together like you and your children. My daddy works all the time and my momma does too," he said. "There's nothing wrong with family getting together every once and awhile. I never had children. I guess God said I don't need any. I've never been married and just can keep a job around here," said the young man. Mr. Will looked at the man and said, "You mean to tell me that getting a wife, children and a job is a hard thing for you to do! Man, you can have anything you want. You just don't want anything! If you pray and give your life to God, He will give you whatever you desire. You got to leave everything in God's hand. I prayed for my wife, and she's a good woman, too. Now, when you pray for a woman, don't pray for just any woman. Pray for a woman who is a praying woman. All women don't know how to pray! Some of them pray for things. They want a pretty man, pretty house, a pretty car, and clothes.

Then, they don't know how to take care of all that stuff. Now take your daddy! He's got a good woman, too. Your people are hard-working people. They took care of their children and their home. I know your momma is a praying woman, but I don't know about your dad's prayer life," Mr. Will said, as they both looked at each other and smiled. They shook hands and the young man left walking down the road.

Mr. Will watered his flowers and walked to the back yard to pray. Lord, I thank you for this day. I thank you for my family. Thank you for this beautiful gathering. Bless my children and my grandchildren, Lord! Bless my wife and keep her safe from all harm and danger. I know, Father, that I'm not what you want me to be, but I have done my best. Don't hold it against me when I don't do everything right. I'm just a man, who was raised by a man, who didn't know how to raise me as a man. Sometimes, I get emotional and cry! I cry, but I feel good crying. It relieves me of all fear inside. I don't have a doubt that everything is going to be alright. This is my evening prayer. Thank You Jesus, Amen.

CHAPTER 18

Weeks passed and the weather changed.

Mr. Will got up early this morning. He skipped breakfast. He had too much on his "to do" list. People from all over town had called for apples. This year was going to be a prosperous year.

Some of the neighborhood children had thrown sticks in the tree to get apples. He never minded them getting apples, but they would leave their sticks for him to pick up. There were about six children standing in the road watching the apple tree.

"Granddaddy, Granddaddy," they yelled. "Can we have some of your apples?" Mr. Will walked near where they were. "You children come here. Did you all throw sticks at my tree?" he asked. All the children looked at each other. One of the boys answered, "Yes." The other children didn't have anything to say. They stood there looking at each other. "I don't mind you coming in the yard to pick apples off the grass, but don't throw sticks at my tree. Granddaddy is an old man now. I can't bend over like I once have. Old people have to be careful not to fall and break bones," he said to the children as they laughed while looking at each other.

"We got it, Granddaddy. Do you want us to help you pick some of the apples off the ground? We know how to do it! We can tell the bad from the good ones," said one little girl. Mr. Will allowed them to help. He loved all the neighborhood kids and they loved him.

Afternoon Lunchtime

The house was quiet after lunch. Mrs. Olivia was reading her noon scriptures. The phone rang as Mr. Will was getting up from the table. "Hello, who is this? Speak up, please. I can't understand you. Let me get my wife. She can understand a little better than me," he said to the person on the phone. Mrs. Olivia took the phone and said, "You don't mean it. When did he go? Tell him we are praying for him and God will beat us there," she said to the caller.

She put the phone down and looked at her husband and said, "Pa, we got bad news. Our son is in the hospital and it doesn't look good. The doctors have given him up. I want you to sit down and listen to me. You know that we didn't come here to stay. We all got to go sooner or later. He wants to come home and pass away with his family and friends. I guess he can stay here until the time comes. He's on his way tonight. I don't want you to worry about anything. We must listen to God and obey His will. It's going to come a time when all our children must leave this world, whether we are here or not. It's going to happen. Some parents must bury their children and sometimes the children must bury their parents. God will take care of us and give us strength to bear our pain," she said as she stood over her husband and rubbed his back.

Mr. Will was so heartbroken. He wiped his eyes and said, "I'm not surprised. I knew something was going to happen. I asked the Lord to show me what it was. Every time one of my friends or family passes away, the apple tree loses a limb. I can feel it happening. Part of me is going away and I will never see it again. Just like that tree," he told his wife.

Six Weeks Later

Mr. Will and Mrs. Olivia had another family gathering. This one has hit home. Their son was their first child to pass away. The other children got together and made all the arrangements. They all felt that their daddy was too heartbroken to sing. Other family members had a part on the program. Mr. Will was strong when time came to view the body. Mrs. Olivia held him up as they proceeded to their seats. Everyone in town knew Mr. Will and his family. They brought flowers, money, food, and cards to show their condolences.

After the burial, everyone stopped by the home. Mrs. Olivia begged their friends and family to take the food and drinks with them. The girls cleaned the house before leaving, while the boys entertained their daddy and friends outside. They talked about the good old days and about the things their brother would do.

"He was my son, you know. All of you boys are part of me, and I love you so much. I don't wish this on nobody," said Mr. Will. "A father shouldn't have to bury his sons. I'm just thankful that nobody killed him. He didn't die from an overdose of drugs and he didn't kill himself, but God took him. He was sick, and when the time came, he gave his life. He wanted to leave this world because of his illness. I can feel for a person like that. I'm just sorry that he didn't live long enough to see his children grow up and see his grandchildren before he passed away. If the Bible is true, he will see them with his spiritual eyes, not in the flesh," he cried thinking about his son.

The Next Month

Apples, apples, apples! Mr. Will made a sign for the friends who always bought his apples. People came from miles away. His close friends would come early in the morning to pick their own apples.

Minnie was his closest friend! They were like siblings. If you didn't know any better, you would have thought they were kin. Minnie would watch Mr. Will's every step. She wanted everything Mr. Will had. If he bought a new flower for his garden, she wanted one too. Minnie was good at baking and cooking. She could bake a pie like no other—except Mr. Will!

Minnie would walk to the apple tree and get her own apples. She didn't wait to be invited. When Mr. Will got up and went outside, Minnie was walking home with a bag of apples. "Hey, Will, she yelled. It's a beautiful day today! I'm going to make me a dumpling with these apples. I'll let you know when it's ready. I want you to taste it while it's hot. It's a new recipe my church member gave me," she said as she walked across the road to her house. Mr. Will yelled back and said he would see her later.

A Few Hours Later

His children were on their way home to discuss his upcoming birthday. They wanted to have the best party ever. This was his 80th birthday. As he walked in the house, Mrs. Olivia was preparing dinner.

"Pa, you know the children are coming home today. I don't want you to drink your little water! When they get here, they want to do the talking, because they got to get back on the road before dark," she said as she continued to wash the dishes. He gave her a look that would crack the ceiling.

"Honey, I know what I'm doing. That little drink makes me feel good. There's nothing wrong with me taking a little drink! Everybody needs a shot ever now and then! When my boys come, I like to have something to give them. I don't see them like I want to, so when we get together, we have fun while you and the girls laugh and talk in the house," he said as he got up and gave her a kiss. Mrs. Olivia turned around and gave him a hug.

One by one, the cars pulled in the driveway. Their oldest girl was always the first to arrive. The other girls came in the side door where their dad was. All the boys came at the same time. Mr. Will was beside himself! All his tall, handsome boys gathered around him, hugging him and telling him how good he looked. Everyone went to the living room to discuss plans for the party. The girls would do all the decorating. One of the girls volunteered to make the guest list. The other girls made the menu.

Mrs. Olivia was excited about her favorite cousins coming from South Carolina. There would be over a hundred people at this party! One of the boys passed a note to his brothers. He wanted to get their daddy a new suit with a shirt and tie to go with it. Navy blue with a gold tie and white shirt would be the gift. Everyone agreed on the plans. Mrs. Olivia had prepared dinner, and it was now prayer time. They all made a circle around the kitchen table while their mother led the prayer.

They all got their food and then someone came to the door. It was Minnie! "Come on in, girl. You brought my dumplings just in time," yelled Mr. Will. Minnie had a large pot filled with apple dumplings. All the children greeted Minnie and asked about her family. She didn't stay too long because her children were home too. "You know, Will. I love all your children. I don't know which one I love the best. All of them are sweet," said Minnie. "The Lord gave us a big family. He knew what He was doing. I thank God every day for my children. I'm just like Will; I'm going to praise my pond while I can, so when I'm gone on, it will be up to them to keep the praising going. We had a hard time raising our children. I was glad I had my momma to help me with mine. Will, you and Olivia had it a little easier than me. You two were able to work and keep your children fed, but mom and I didn't have any one but us and the good Lord. I'm thankful for everything he did for me. If I had to do it again, I don't think I would change a thing," she said as she stood at the door to go home.

"Girl, you know we had it hard back then, but God blessed us to make it this far," said Mr. Will. "All our children are grown and if I live to see April, I will be 80 years old. You not too far behind, are you? Minnie looked at Mr. Will and said, "We are the same age. You don't look like you are 80!" Mr. Will smiled and started bragging. "Well, you know I've been a good-looking man all my life. I was born good looking. My momma said when I was born, I had curls in my hair so big, that the only thing she had to do was set my curls with her fingers. I can't help it! The women folks think I'm a good-looking guy, but I don't pay them any attention. I love my wife and no other woman alive will ever take her place. When I say the Lord's been good to me, I mean it with all I got. He blessed me and my wife with good looks, and my children are beautiful, all of them. I don't have not one ugly kid. If anybody tell you that one of them are ugly, they tells' a lie," said Mr Will. Minnie stood at the door and said, "Well, I better go on that one! I hope you children have a safe trip back to your homes. Will, I'll see you later!"

Later that Evening

All the children had left. Mrs. Olivia sat at the table to read her Bible. Mr. Will was in his chair taking a nap. Mrs. Olivia stop reading for a second. She thought she heard someone at the back door. She got up and looked out the window. It was Snow. He was wobbling as he tried to step up on the porch. There was something wrong with him. And, suddenly, he fell to the ground. His mouth was opened, and blood was flowing from his nose. She woke Mr. Will and told him to come see about Snow. "Oh, my God! My dog is dead." He picked Snow up in his arms and took him to the back yard. "I have to call the Animal Hospital. They will come and get him. I'll have to pay a little something, but I don't mind. I'm going to let them bury him. He's been a good dog. I'll never get another smart dog like Snow. I trained him from a puppy. I love my dog! He will be missed," cried Mr. Will.

The next day, the Animal Control came and got Snow's body. Mr. Will went with them. He wanted to make sure they put him away decently. As he was driving back home from the hospital, he looked back and cried, "Lord, everybody close to me are leaving me behind. I know we all have a date to be born and a date to leave this world. I know You don't make any mistakes, but I get sad sometimes. I think about all my buddies who are gone. I miss them so much, Lord."

Mrs. Olivia walked to the driveway to meet Mr. Will. She opened the car door for him and said, "Pa, how much did it cost you? Burying a dog should be cheaper than burying a person." He didn't say anything. She could tell that he had been crying.

"Don't you get sick worrying about that dog. I miss him too! He was getting too old. He couldn't run and play anymore. Animals are like human beings. Then want people to pay them some attention. You old, the dog old, and I know I'm not going outside to play with him. Come on in the house and cool yourself off. You got so much to do around this house, you will soon forget about Snow. Do you want me to call the children and tell them about him?" Mrs. Olivia asked. Mr. Will nodded. Then he went to his room and laid on the bed.

CHAPTER 19

The Next Day

Mr. Will got up early. His customers were coming to get more apples. He decided to make more apple pies. He made his grocery list. Mrs. Olivia wanted to go with him this time. As they entered the grocery store, he saw his brother. They greeted each other and shared ideas about the apples.

"Will, do you know how to make apple wine?" his brother asked. "Man, I tasted some wine that one of my old buddies made, and it was good!" said Mr. Will. "If you are going back home now, I can meet you there and I'll show you what to do," his brother said, as he was leaving the store.

Mr. Will and Mrs. Olivia got everything they needed and head back home. When they arrived, his brother was sitting on the picnic table. He had picked a bucket full of apples. "When you go in the house, bring a pencil and a sheet of paper. I have to write everything down for you," he told Mr. Will, as they were getting out of the car. The two brothers sat down at the table and made their recipe for apple wine.

One Hour Later

Mr. Will and his brother got the bucket of apples. They washed them and removed all the stems and leaves. "What we need to do is, put the apples in the bucket and cover them tightly. They got to set for a week. Don't open them until I come up here. I got to see if they are working—

that means they are getting right for wine," he told Mr. Will.

When his brother left, Mr. Will bagged apples for his friends. People came from the countryside. They traveled from other counties. Mr. Will and Mrs. Olivia peeled apples all afternoon. They had twelve pie shells ready for the oven.

They heard a knock at the door. It was Edward. Mr. Will hadn't seen him in a while. Mr. Edward washed his hands to help his friend make pies. "I need about 10 pies for myself, Will. I got some people on the other street who want a pie. Do you think you have enough for me today, or do I have to wait until tomorrow?" he asked. "I think we'll have enough! I can put some of these apples in a bowl. The only thing we need to do now, is add the sugar and seasonings," said Mr. Will. Edward stirred the apple mixture and poured it in the pie shells. The oven could only bake four pies at a time.

"You know, me and my brother are making some wine. We got it covered and waiting for it to work. He told me it had to set for a week. What do you think?" Mr. Will asked his friend. Edward went outside to see the container with the apples. "How long have they been out here?" he asked. "Only about two hours," said Mr. Will. "This is my first wine making project! You made some grape wine last year and it didn't take that long. You think my brother know what he's talking about? He will tell me anything, and think I'm going to believe it, too!" said Mr. Will. Edward didn't say anything. He didn't want to bother with making apple wine. He always made grape wine. It was the best in the county and Mr. Will knew it, too!

The two men went in the house to check on the pies. Mrs. Olivia had taken them out the oven. "Are they ready, Honey?" asked Mr. Will. She nodded. She placed the pies on the counter. Mr. Will and Edward wrapped each pie with foil. Mrs. Olivia got on the phone to call the people who ordered the pies. "How much did you say the pies were, Pa?" Mr. Will got his writing pad and wrote they were $10 each. "You know what? We should have made some dried apples," said Mr. Will. "They are easy to make. All we need to do is slice the apples and lay them outside on something flat and let the sun dry them. When they're dry, put them in a zip-lock bag and put the price on them. What do you think about that?" he asked his wife and Edward. Mrs. Olivia didn't say a word and Edward started out the door. "I'm going to see you later, Will! I have stayed too long. If I don't leave now, you will have me over here all night long. I got to go home and check on my old lady," he said as he walked out the door. "Tell your wife I said hello and stay with the Lord," said Mr. Will. Edward said he would and got in his truck to go home.

Later that Evening

Everyone came and got their pies. Mr. Will made $50 profit. Mrs. Olivia put the money in her money bag.

It had been a long day. They were tired and wanted to rest. Mrs. Olivia cleaned the kitchen and helped her husband get ready for bed. They both said the evening prayer. "Pa, did you thank the Lord for the money we made today?" asked Mrs. Olivia. "Don't ever forget the Lord! He was the one who provided for us. I'm going to put some extra change aside to give to the Lord, Sunday. He is so good to us! Whoever thought we would be making pies at this age. Most people our age are sitting around the house knitting or playing games, but we are still picking apples and making pies. After this year, I think we should give it up. We're getting too old now. Our children need to be doing more with these apples. You need to show them how to bake and make dried apples. Pa, are you listening to me?" she asked.

Mr. Will didn't hear a word she said. He was fast asleep. She pulled the covers over him and removed his glasses. *"Lord, this man can't stop working. I guess, if he stops now, he will die. He's been working all his life. He's been a good Pa to his children and me, but I don't want to keep peeling apples every year. I need to go out and visit some of these sick people and give them the Word. Just give me strength Lord, to keep up with this man,"* she prayed, as she turned over in her bed for the night.

CHAPTER 20

I t was early Monday morning. Mr. Will was up and waiting for his brother. He went outside to get the bucket of apples. He couldn't wait to see what was going on inside. When he lifted the bucket up, it felt lighter for some reason. He put the bucket on the picnic table as his brother drove in the yard.

"Hey, man! I took the bucket out so we can see what's going on with these apples! The bucket feels lighter. We had this thing full of apples. Should it be like this?" he asked. His brother said, "No! We got to be careful! I hope the apples didn't make a film on top of the lid! If it did, we're in trouble! Mr. Will looked at his brother and said, "What you mean, *we* are in trouble? You going to be in trouble because you told me you knew how to make wine. I don't want you to waste my good apples! I could have sold these apples, but no, you wanted to make wine," Mr. Will fussed.

His brother braced himself. He opened the bucket carefully. When he looked in the bucket, the juice was foaming white soapy juice. It was making a humming sound! It filled the top and started running out of the bucket!

"Run, Will! Run for your life! I think we made a bomb! It won't stop running and I don't see any apples!" Mr. Will started running towards the house. The juice was running off the table and onto the ground. It ran until all the foam was gone. "Are you alright, Will?" asked his brother. By now, Mr. Will was standing on the front porch. He ran so fast he forgot his hat on the table! "Yeah man, I'm alright! What happened? I have never seen anything like that before!" said Mr. Will. His brother was on top of his car hood. He ran so fast he didn't remember jumping on the car. "I don't know! I think it has stopped foaming!" said his brother.

He got off the car and went over to the bucket. "Come here man! Look!" his brother said. "I see juice in the bucket! I think we have made wine! It looks like wine! It smells like wine, too," he said, as he stuck his finger in the bucket to taste it. "Oh, boy! This is good! Bring me a strainer, so we can pour the juice in this jar," his brother said. Mr. Will went inside the house to get the strainer. He held the jar and strainer while his brother poured the juice from the bucket. "It's wine! I can smell it, and it tastes good too! I can't believe we made wine! We are going to be rich!" he said to Mr. Will. The brothers filled 2-quart jars with the wine. They decided to taste again to make sure it was strong enough. They tasted a cup full. Then, they tasted another cup full, and another cup full. Mr. Will tasted so much he couldn't get up from the table.

He laughed when there was nothing funny. He talked about his dog and cried. He wanted to see his son who passed away. He wanted to hug and kiss his brother! He yelled for Mrs. Olivia to come outside. His brother put his head down on the table. He couldn't move! Mrs. Olivia came running. "Lord, what in the world has this man done," she said as she tried to wake her brother-in-law and take the cup from Mr. Will. "Pa, can you walk?" Mr. Will didn't say a word.

She took him by the hand and helped him up. He walked with her to the front door. She guided him to his bed. "Pa, you know better than to sit out there and drink all that juice! How much did you drink?" she asked, but Mr. Will was quiet. After she got him in the bed, she went outside to wake his brother. But, when she got outside, he was driving away in his car. "Jesus, please Lord! Don't let that boy run into nothing," she prayed. She cleared the table. She smelled the cups that they were drinking from and took them in the house. "My goodness! I wouldn't drink this stuff if someone paid me to," thought Mrs. Olivia. "It smells bad! I wonder, what did they put in where to make it smell so bad?" she thought, as she cleaned the table and put the jars of wine away in Mr. Will's closet.

The Next Day

Cleaning the yard was going to be a great task for Mr. Will. He woke up with a bad headache! It took him a while to get started. Mrs. Olivia had to call him several times this morning. She listened for him to come out of the bedroom. He came a few minutes later. He wore his bedroom shoes, which was unusual. He still wore his pajama shirt, which he thought was his shirt. "Good morning, Pa! Do you want coffee this morning?" she asked. He didn't speak. He just shook his head and smiled. "What's so funny, Pa?" she asked, laughing at her husband. "Your head still hurting? What are you doing with your pajama top on? And look at your feet! Where are your shoes? You're all turned around, today. I don't think you need to drink anymore of your wine. If it makes you act like this, you and your brother should make pies and leave the wine making for Edward," she said as she smiled at Mr. Will and he smiled back.

Mrs. Olivia prepared his breakfast and laid his clothes out for the day. After getting dressed, Mr. Will walked outside and sat down on the table. He thought to himself, "What was I thinking about, to let that boy talk me into drinking all that wine? He really made a bomb! It blew us away, yesterday! I hope he made it home okay!"

Mrs. Olivia came outside with the phone. It was a call from the children. The birthday party was going to start at 5 p.m. on Saturday. There would be over 100 family members and friends there. Mr. Will was excited about the party. "Honey bring me a cup of black coffee! I got to wake up, so I can clean this yard. Do we have enough pies for Saturday?" he asked his wife. She looked at him and said, "Don't you worry about having pies at the party. The Baby told you they were going to make the menu. All we have to do is be there!" He told his wife that he wanted her to wear a beautiful dress for the party. He loved to see her in pink. She had several pink dresses and a pink pants suit. "I know what I want to wear! You just make sure you have your suit out the cleaners," said Mrs. Olivia.

Mr. Will got busy mowing the lawn. He worked in his garden. He looked at Snow's doghouse. He decided to give it to one of the children in the neighborhood. The yard was clean from front to back! He washed his car and his truck. "Lord, that man is working like a bee today! I hope he is alright!" thought Mrs. Olivia. "Pa, do you want something to drink? It's hot out there!" Mrs. Olivia said, as she walked to the back yard to check on him. "No, I'm alright! I got to finish before dark. I need to go to the grocery store. Do you want to ride with me?" he asked. He stopped for a few minutes and changed his clothes. Mrs. Olivia wrote his grocery list. The couple drove to the store and enjoyed the rest of their evening.

CHAPTER 21

I t was finally time for Mr. Will and his wife to get ready for the party. She told him to take his bath first because it always took him longer in the bathroom. "Pa, I'm going to lay your clothes on the bed and your shoes are in the living room. You don't have to run all the water in the county, save some for the folks on the other street!" she teased. She had to approach him with humor whenever he was going somewhere. Something about getting dressed up would make him nervous.

"Baby, let me do like I want to do. I'm dirty and sweaty from mowing the lawn. Have you seen my shaving kit? I don't see my eyebrow pencil! Would you please hand me my soap? I forgot my bath cloth and towel," he said, standing in the bathroom with his robe on! Mrs. Olivia gave him a towel and bath cloth. She reminded him that his soap was in the shower.

Thirty minutes later, Mr. Will was getting dressed. Mrs. Olivia got a phone call from one of the girls saying they were on their way to pick up their parents. The birthday boy was ready! He was dressed in a gray suit that the boys gave him for Father's Day. He was undecided about the color of the tie he should wear. "Honey, does this blue tie go with my suit and shirt?" he asked. He wanted to get his wife's opinion because she was good at matching colors. "Yes, Pa. That looks good! I can hear everyone saying, 'Mr. Will is sharp as a tack. If you touch him; you might get stuck!' she said, as they both laughed.

The girls arrived. Mrs. Olivia opened the door. "Hello, Mother! Hi, Daddy! Oh, you two look like a million bucks! Mom, your hair is beautiful. Daddy let me fix your tie! Happy Birthday, to my daddy! I'm so thankful that the Lord has allowed you to see eighty years old! Daddy, you look so good! I'm glad you are taking good care of him, Mom," their daughters said, as they kissed and hugged their parents.

"It's time to go," the girls said. Everyone got in their own cars and drove to the party. When they arrived, the parking lot was full. It was decorated with balloons and a huge sign that read, "HAPPY BIRTHDAY!" When they went inside, all their children had a seat at the special guest table. When Mr. Will looked around to see all of his guests, he saw one of his favorite cousins. "Oh, my goodness. Is that you girl? I haven't seen you in months," he said, as they both stood up to hug each other. It was Aggie! She was the only cousin on his father's side. They visited each other often, until their health started failing.

There were so many people at the party! The oldest son and daughter were the "Masters of Ceremony." Another son led the prayer, and the other two greeted the guests and thanked everyone for coming.

It was time to toast Mr. Will! There was only one person who could describe him, and that was one of his best friends. Edward stood up and walked to the front of the room. He fixed his coat and tie. He rubbed the top of his head and cleared his throat and said, "I would like to thank you children for giving me the pleasure of expressing my feelings about my buddy over there. Most of you don't know, but Will and I were raised up in the country, about three miles east of town. We went to school together and then off to the Army. I want you all to know that I love that man! Now, I'm not funny or anything like that, but you know what I mean. He is like a brother to me. We get along better than some brothers. He is fun to be around. We never argue. If he says something that I don't like, well, I just tell him how I feel about it and then I go home. That's the way friends should be. I hope he lives to see many more birthdays. You children really did a great job on his celebration. Happy Birthday to my friend! May God bless both of you," said Edward.

Everyone stood and clapped for Edward. When he walked back to his seat, he grabbed Mr. Will and gave him a big hug. Mr. Will wiped his eyes with his handkerchief and took his seat. All the children stood up and wished their daddy a happy birthday. They gave him cards with money, baskets of flowers, beautifully wrapped presents, and a money tree. Each branch was full of ten dollar bills! Mr. Will was speechless. He cried as the children made over him. The food was served by the grandchildren, who acted as waitresses and waiters. When dinner was over, Mr. Will and Mrs. Olivia cut the cake.

Next, it was time for entertainment. The boys turned the music up and all the children and grandchildren got on the dance floor. Everyone who could walk was on the floor. Mr. Will danced with each one of his girls, then it was Mrs. Olivia's turn. She always told people her mom didn't allow her to dance, but when Mr. Will asked her to get up, she did! "Come on Honey, all you got to do is move your feet when I move mine. Just stand here and let me lead you," he said, as he hugged his wife around her waist with one hand and held her hand with the other. The grandchildren were excited to see their grandparents dancing. They knew Mr. Will could dance but their grandma never tried to dance. The only thing they ever saw her do was read her Bible.

Finally, the party was over. It was time to go home. The children gathered all the gifts and left-over food. All the children followed their parents home to help with the gifts and put the food away. Mrs. Olivia made sure to tell her children to call when they got home. She worried about them on the dark road at night because they had a long ride home.

The house was quiet. Mr. Will took off his clothes to get ready for bed. "I'm telling you, Honey! I had a good time tonight," said Mr. Will, beaming. "My babies really showed off and showed out! Everything was just beautiful. My grand babies enjoyed themselves too. Those boys did a good job. The girls planned that party and made a menu that was fit for a king! They all worked together on this one! I hope the Lord will let me see many more birthdays, but I doubt it. I feel like this is going to be my last birthday," he said, as Mrs. Olivia untied his shoes.

"You don't know what the Lord's going to do, Pa. If you take your vitamins and eat right, you might live to see a hundred," she said as she walked to the bedroom. Mr. Will held his head back on the chair. He closed his eyes and started praying.

"I thank you Lord, for everything you have done for me. You been so good to my family. I thank you for it! You brought me from a mighty long way. All through the storms of life. All the mistakes I've made. You forgave me and saved my soul. I'm not worried about a thing tonight. I'm happy in my soul. If I don't wake up in the morning, I know you will take me up to glory. So many of my children won't live to see 80 like me. But bless them to see another year. And, if it's your will Lord, show me the end of my days. I love you, Lord. In Your Holy name I pray. Amen."

CHAPTER 22

The Next Month

All the apples were gone. Mrs. Olivia sliced the last bucket of apples to freeze. The garden spot was all grown over with weeds and dead grass. Mr. Will walked to the back yard to see what needed his attention first—the garden spot or the apple tree.

One of his grandsons drove in the driveway. He sat down on the picnic table. He saw Mr. Will walking and yelled, "Hey, Granddaddy. What are you doing?" Mr. Will greeted him with a hug and said, "I need to cut this hill down. The grass is getting too high. But I don't want to worry you boys with something I can do myself."

The boy got up and went around the house to see what he was talking about. "Granddaddy, I'll cut it for you. I don't want you to fall," he said. Mr. Will refused to let the boy help. He wanted to do it himself. "Come on, Granddaddy. Give me the mower. It won't take but a minute to do it," he begged. Mr. Will finally gave in. His grandson cut the grass on the hill and offered to trim the apple tree, too.

"No, you don't have to bother with the tree. It needs to be trimmed, but I'll do that next month," said Mr. Will. "You got to know what you're doing when you're working with my tree. That tree is just like me—old and needs a lot of tender loving care," he told the boy as they laughed. When Mr. Will stood up, he staggered. "Granddaddy are you alright?" the boy asked, grabbing Mr. Will's arm to keep him from falling. "I don't know, son. I don't feel well. Go get your Grandma," he said.

The boy ran to the house to get Mrs. Olivia. She looked at Mr. Will and knew something was wrong. He couldn't walk by himself. She and her grandson got him in the house. They took him to the bedroom. Mrs. Olivia called the doctor. The doctor wanted them to call the Emergency Medic to bring him to the hospital. She also called all the children to let them know.

One Hour Later

All the children went to the hospital with Mrs. Olivia. The news wasn't good. The doctor told them that Mr. Will had only six to 12 months to live. The family got together and asked Mr. Will what he wanted to do after leaving the hospital. They agreed to bring him home to pass away.

Getting prepared for a patient in the home was going to be a great task. The children decided to take days at a time to help their mom care for their dad.

The Next Day

All of Mr. Will's friends came by to see him. They offered to help in any way that was needed. Edward was the first person to come and sit with him. He told Mrs. Olivia that he would stay with him any time.

Everyone was on schedule. The girls came during the week and the boys on the weekend. Mr. Will was a good patient. He wanted to be entertained all the time. He loved playing cards with the boys and some of his church buddies. His appetite was good. He loved shrimp and oyster soup. Mrs. Olivia cooked every day and made the soup on Saturdays.

The children had to dress him every day. He refused to wear his pajamas during the day, so Mrs. Olivia would lay out a set of clothes for him each day. The girls didn't like that idea, but she was okay with it. She loved her husband and wanted him to be comfortable. "Mom, you don't have to change dad's clothes every day. That's too much washing! We don't want you to wear yourself out. You have to cook three times a day and keep the house clean," said one of the girls. Mrs. Olivia was thankful that they were concerned about her, but it didn't matter, she was going to do what she saw fit to do for her husband.

The doctor was coming to see Mr. Will the next day. The family needed equipment for their dad. Most of the grandchildren were excited to help with the wheelchair and the lift. Mr. Will had the best caregivers ever! He was a patient that didn't complain! Whatever they told him to do, he was willing.

Later that evening, his brother came by to see him. "Man, if you drink some of that wine we made, you'll get up and start walking again!" his brother said, laughing. He rubbed Mr. Will's head and held his hand. "How are you doing today? I had to come see you before your bedtime and get back home before dark," his brother said. Mr. Will looked at him and laughed. He was in a good mood! His brother always played cards with him, but it was hard to get him to come visit when Mr. Will was up and going. He stayed too busy for his brother. It was such a treat to have his brother there! The two of them talked and laughed about the good old days. Mrs. Olivia made soup and sandwiches for dinner. She prepared extra for his brother.

"Pa, do you want some ice cream? I have cake, too!" said Mrs. Olivia. Mr. Will said he did, but he wanted his brother to eat it, too. "No ice cream for me! I'll take some cake before I leave," his brother said. They enjoyed each other's company until Mr. Will fell asleep. Mrs. Olivia closed the door and his brother went home.

The Next Day

All the equipment had arrived. Mr. Will and Mrs. Olivia's sons were coming home today. Breakfast was prepared and the house was cleaned. Mrs. Olivia was getting ready to do her laundry. She heard a car outside. It was their sons.

"Hey, son! Come on in and get something to eat. Your daddy isn't dressed yet, but he's awake. He wants to go outside today. He's been talking about that apple tree. I told him you couldn't stay long because you all have to go to work," she said.

The boys got their dad up and rolled him outside. He wanted to see his apple tree. Mr. Will looked at the tree and said, "You know son, this tree is getting old. I bought this tree at the Super-Mart and Robert planted it for me. I prayed about this tree and God answered my prayers. The only thing I wanted to do was to make people happy by giving them something they enjoyed. I made pies for many people and made good money, too. People would come from miles just to get some of my apples. Now your mom and me are tired. The only thing I want to do now is to rest and live one day at a time."

He continued. "I want you boys to do something for me. Take the seeds from some of these apples and dry them out. Place the seeds in a paper bag. Put them in a safe place, like your closet or pantry. Don't bother the seeds but keep them there to give to your children. Teach them how to plant the seeds and then, they will have their own apple tree. This tree is part of me. I will live a long time through this tree. Every time your children look at their tree, they will think of me," said Mr. Will. "The Lord has been good to me and your momma. I am so proud of all you boys. I want you to let your children know what kind of daddy you had. I wasn't perfect. I made a lot of mistakes during my time on this Earth, but God kept me from all harm and danger. Sometimes, I just sit and cry. Your momma looks at me and ask me what's wrong, I don't say anything, I don't want to worry her with my pain of leaving here. She has been a good wife and mother. The Lord sure blessed me with that woman. If I had to do it all over again, I would marry her the second go around. You boys have wonderful wives too! Teach your boys how to choose a wife; don't look for that outer beauty, pray and ask God is that the woman for them. Get a clean woman with a clean spiritual heart. And then, you boys must treat her with all respect; not respect her because she is a woman. Respect her because she belongs to God. If you do like I say, you will be alright. I don't have no doubt that you will live a long and beautiful life like I have," said Mr. Will. His sons just nodded.

"That's enough about me!" said Mr. Will. "Do you see that big limb on the right side of that tree? It has a split in it. That split isn't going to mend back to the tree. It is going to break off and when it does, you need to throw it away. It has no more value. All the life will be gone. That's what I want you to do when it falls. Every time you come home, come back here and check that limb. I won't be able to come out here every time you come but keep watching it for me. You will know what to do," cried Mr. Will, as he poured out his heart to his boys.

The boys took Mr. Will back inside. It was time for them to get on the road to go home. Mrs. Olivia gave them each a frozen apple pie for their wives. "Don't you eat it before you get home. If you put it in the trunk of your car, it will stay cold. Tell the babies we said hey and kiss your wife with love. Take the Lord with you on that dangerous highway back home," she said as the boys got in the car.

Later that Day

Mrs. Olivia prepared lunch for her husband. After his noon nap, one of his neighbors came by to visit with him. "Hey in here!" he said as he stuck his head in the front door. "Anybody home! I'm coming in!" Mrs. Olivia came to the door. It was Mr. Will's friend who always fixed the plumbing. "Come on in! Will is in the first bedroom to your right. He's not asleep, he'll be glad to see you," she said.

The young man went to Mr. Will's room. "Man, you need to get out this bed! You look like the picture of health. I need some plums and peaches!" he said as he pulled a chair from the corner of the room. "I thought you was one of my boys!" said Mr. Will. "What's going on with you, today? I just got back in the bed a few hours ago. My boys came and I feel a little tired. I guess I stayed up too long," Mr. Will said.

The man took his cap off and started crying. "Will, I want you to know how much I love you man. You have been a father to me and my brother," he said as he wept. "My daddy died when we were teenagers, and there hasn't been another man in our life like you. You have been a good friend to me. I can come over here anytime and you never talk down to me. I know I drink and it's a habit. I can do better, and I will! I just need to get rid of some of my no-good friends! They drink and that causes me to drink, too. It's nothing but peer pressure. You remember what you told me about that word! You said, pressure is when you push something, and peer was the person pushing. You told me don't ever let a person push you in front, when they push you in front they are trying to hold you back from doing what's right, but when they push you from the back, they push you to higher heights. A man can be pushed to fall, and a man can be pushed to go forward. You got a lot of wisdom. I love you, man. That's why I like being around you. If all old men would talk to the younger men like you do, this would be a better world for us. I see you're nodding! I'm leaving and let you get some rest," said his friend.

Mr. Will opened one eye and said, "I'm not sleep. I heard every word you said. You are a fine young man. When I am gone, I want you to keep coming by to visit with my wife. You can get some plums off the tree, but don't take all of them like you been doing. If you see anything that needs to be fixed, fix it and you know my boys will pay you. Always check with my baby boy first—he's got all the money," Mr. Will said smiling.

The young man gave Mr. Will a hug and promised to come by again.

CHAPTER 23

The Next Month

Mr. Will grew sicker and was admitted to the hospital. All the children were called. Mrs. Olivia was with him every moment. He didn't want the nurses to feed him or give him a bath. Whenever they asked, he would tell them that his wife was coming and would do it. The girls came to the hospital every day to relieve their mother, but she didn't want to leave his side. Mr. Will had good days and bad. His appetite wasn't the best, so, Mrs. Olivia fed him soups and warm milk.

The doctor came in after breakfast. "Mr. Will, how are you doing today? I see that your wife is taking good care of you, and your children are here to give their support. What else can a man of your character ask for?" he said, as he smiled at Mr. Will.

"I'm thankful, Doc. I'm in the Lord's hand now," said Mr. Will. "I'm not afraid to die. My mother and father had to die. Most of my friends are gone on. Dying isn't a bad thing! If you know what you know and who you know, you're be alright," said Mr. Will. "Have I ever told you about when I went to war? I was in World War 2. On my 18th birthday, I enlisted in the Navy. I was a young man who had never been out of this county. You know, we were segregated back then. But white people didn't bother me. Some of my best buddies were white. I have always been the type of person who would speak my mind. If they didn't like what I said, I said it anyways. I love people. I believe that's why the good Lord let me stay here this long. Doc, I don't want you to keep nothing from me and my family. I know you don't know when I'm leaving here, because nobody knows that but the good Master in heaven!" he said, as the doctor examined him.

Mrs. Olivia sat quietly and let the doctor and her husband chat. Mr. Will was very talkative and seem to be doing as well as expected. When Mrs. Olivia got a chance, she interrupted the conversation and asked, "Do you think my husband will be able to go home soon? We have a hospital bed and wheelchair. My girls will be there to help. I know how to take care of the sick! My mom was sick when I was fourteen. I had to lift her and turn her over in the bed. All my relatives were bedridden and me and my family helped them! Do you think he can go home?"

The doctor looked at Mrs. Olivia. He knew that the stress from taking care of her husband was getting to her. He looked at her and smiled, "Mrs. Olivia, you have been an amazing wife and mother. You must take care of yourself now. I would love for you to go home and get some rest in your own bed, but I know how you feel about your husband. I think we'd better keep him here with us for a few more days, and then, if he wants too, he can go home."

Mr. Will looked at the doctor and said, "Thank you, Doc! I agree with you. I think I'll be better off in here where all these beautiful nurses are. I like when they come in here and smile at me. I have always loved beautiful women. When I saw my wife for the first time, I knew she was mine. She was beautiful then and she is beautiful now!" The doctor finished examining Mr. Will and told him that he would be back in the morning.

The Next Day

Mrs. Olivia went to sleep on a long sleeper's chair. When she awoke, she noticed that her husband wasn't moving. She leaned down to his chest to see if he was breathing. She felt his forehead and then his feet and hands and said, "Oh, my God! Pa is gone!"

She walked out into the hallway of the hospital and called for the nurse. The nurses ran to the room. They examined Mr. Will and called for the doctor. Mrs. Olivia sat down in the chair and watched her husband, and asked, "Is he gone?" The nurses didn't answer her. As they waited for the doctor, one of the nurses said, "I think so, Ma'am, but we are going to let the doctor examine him first."

The doctor came in and greeted Mrs. Olivia. He examined Mr. Will and said, "Well, my friend, you have gone on to be with the Lord! Farewell my soldier! Farewell my friend!" He turned to Mrs. Olivia and said, "I'm sorry for your loss and I am thankful for the Lord's gain. Be thankful, Ma'am. This is what he wanted. He was tired. Your family had a jewel! He was a wonderful man. A godly man! He was well loved by many. God makes no mistakes. It was his time to retire from this world. God had no more use for him here. He is in Heaven, now. Are you alright?" he asked Mrs. Olivia, as he consoled her.

She thanked the doctor and all the nurses for what they had done. One of the nurses assisted her with getting in touch with her children. Mr. Will's body was left in the room until the children came to say their goodbyes.

One Hour Later

All the children and their mother gathered around their daddy's bed. They all held hands in prayer. Mrs. Olivia was the strongest, so she led the prayer. *"Our Father! The Father of Abraham! The Father of the Universe! The Father of all your children. We come to give thanks this morning. We come with sorrow in our hearts because we have lost a special loved one. I want to thank you, Lord, for letting me have my husband for over 50 years. Forgive him Lord, for all his wrong doings. Receive him into your kingdom. We know you love him more than we do, so we say, 'thank you.' We magnify your holy name! Now, bless my children. Bless my home. Bless the doctors and the nurses in this hospital. Take care of the sick all over this land. All these blessings we ask in your name. Amen, Amen, Amen!"*

Everyone left the hospital and went home to be with their mother. "Baby, I want all of you to make the arrangements for your daddy," said Mrs. Olivia. "I have the insurance information in my drawer. Your daddy told me what he wanted at his homegoing service. We're not going to have a long service because I don't want to sit for a long time. I would like for one of you to call the pastor. Who can we get to sing a solo for your dad? He always sang at his friends' funerals. Now we need someone to sing for him," she said, as she sat in her husband's chair.

One of the girls suggested that they ask Mr. Ledbetter to sing for their dad. The plan was for one person to call for the soloist and another get in touch with some of the local pastors in the neighborhood. The mortician brought a wreath and stands before the children went home.

People all over town heard about the passing of Mr. Will. They came to give their condolences. They gave cards, food, their time and their prayers. Mrs. Olivia was so tired that she went to bed while the children entertained the guests.

9 p.m. that Night

People were outside on the picnic table. All the children's classmates and their neighborhood friends were there. Mr. Will's brothers and sisters were there. One of his friends suggested that they play a hand of cards in memory of Mr. Will.

When they took the table out, one of the legs was missing. "What happened to the leg on this table?" asked the baby boy. "Are you sure it had four legs when daddy played?" he asked, while laughing and looking around the room at his other brothers. "Yes! Daddy bought this table last year! Well, maybe Robert came and took it away, or maybe, Mr. Tee walked across the street and borrowed it," one of the boys said, as all the men headed for the door to run. "Well, I guess we're not going to play cards after all! Everybody is afraid of Robert and Mr. Tee!" the baby boy said, while watching the men get in the cars. "We'll see you all tomorrow. It's getting late, and I have to go to work tomorrow," said one the men who Mr. Will called his adopted son.

The Next Day

The girls stayed overnight with their mother. One cooked breakfast. One did the laundry. Two of the girls cleaned the house to make it nice for receiving guests. Minnie was the first person to visit Mrs. Olivia. She bought a dish of her favorite chicken and dumplings. Mrs. Olivia asked her to have a seat. As she looked around for a chair, she started crying and said she was going to miss her best friend.

"Well, we all got to leave here. We can't stay," said Mrs. Olivia. "This is not our home. I lost my momma, my pa, my son, and my brothers. I never thought Will would go before me, but I'm glad the Lord planned it that way. If it had been me to go first, Pa would've worried these children to death! You know they all got him spoiled. He would have them doing everything for him. They would have to come live in this house again," Mrs.

Olivia told Minnie.

The ministers arrived. One of the girls opened the door for them. They gave their condolences and slipped a check in Mrs. Olivia's pocket. One of the pastors opened his Bible and read a scripture and another one prayed. "Mr. Will is going to be missed at church. I loved to hear him sing 'The Lord's Prayer.' I always wondered why he didn't sing professionally. But growing up in his time, I guess it was difficult to make it in this small town. He was a good singer," the pastor said. Mrs. Olivia agreed and added, "My husband could play the piano, too! Most of his sisters and brothers could play. They always played hymns on Sunday and the Blues on Saturday. He started a family choir. It was named after him. We traveled to other churches, went to the rest homes, and sang in our friend's home. Yes, my husband was a character! He had a lot of friends; black and white. I'm going to miss him being around the house. People don't realize it, but a piece of a man is better than no man at all."

The ministers agreed to come help with the homegoing service. They prayed for the family before leaving.

The Day of the Funeral

It was a beautiful day. Mrs. Olivia got up early and started getting her clothes ready for the funeral. It was going to be an early funeral, so the family had to be at the house and ready to go. Mrs. Olivia was ready when the family cars arrived. All the family members were in the house waiting for the pastors. Ten minutes later, everyone was in place.

They arrived at the church in thirty minutes. Service started the next hour. The church was packed! There was just enough room in the church for about 20 more people. Mr. Will's homegoing service was the most talked about service in a long time. People who couldn't get in the church stood in the parking lot. They took pictures and videos of the service. There were motorcycle clubs there. The police department and the government officials were there. People who didn't know Mr. Will thought a celebrity had passed away.

During the funeral, all the children got up to thank everyone for attending their father's service. "My dad will be missed greatly. He loved everybody in this town, and I believe you all loved him too. Keep praying for our mom and pray for us too. I know that you who always come by to see Dad won't stop coming to see Mom. We love you all and thank you so much," said one of the boys.

After the funeral, the children took their mother home. It had been a long week for her, and they were glad everything was over.

CHAPTER 24

The Next Month

The weather was getting cooler. Mrs. Olivia was living alone. She missed her husband so much! There was no more getting up early preparing breakfast for him. She missed him walking around the back yard to pray near the apple tree. She kept his clothes. She wanted the children to take what they wanted and give some of them to the local clothes closet.

The children wanted her to keep busy. They made her a schedule for every day of the week. Visiting the county's rest home was an activity she loved. They made sure she kept all her doctor's appointments and continued to go to church each Sunday.

Everything was going as they planned. One day the children called and wanted to come home to tell her about one of Mr. Will's requests. She told them she would stay home and wait for them.

Later that Evening

All the children arrived about the same time. Mrs. Olivia had prepared dinner and insisted that they eat and take a plate home.

Her son said, "Mom, Dad wanted us to do something for him. He didn't tell you about it then, but we can share it with you now. He saved some apple seeds a few months ago. He wanted us to give them to our children for safe keeping. I know we are getting older and our children are leaving for school and some of are having families of their own. I have a bag of seeds that dad gave me. I want you to pray over these seeds. When dad was living, he always prayed near the apple tree. There was something strange about him and that tree. Can we all go outside with the seeds while you pray?"

Mrs. Olivia got up and they all walked outside to the apple tree. When they walked around the house, one of the boys noticed something. "Look! That limb broke off! Daddy told me that it was going to fall off. I wonder, how long has it been out here?" the baby boy asked.

Mrs. Olivia said that the limb was like that the day Mr. Will died. Mrs. Olivia said, "When we came home from the hospital, I looked out the window, thinking about your daddy, and I saw the limb on the ground. I thought someone cut it like that. But now you're telling me that it was already broken. Your daddy was something else! He told me one day that his apple tree was talking to him. I didn't believe what he said because he would talk out of his head when he drank his little water. Do you all think your daddy's spirit is in that tree?" Mrs. Olivia's eyes grew wide as she looked around at her children.

The children were speechless. They all started walking toward the tree. "There's something strange about this tree, now! Look at it! Daddy's skin was withered before he died, and the tree is withering away, too! Mom, how long has this tree looked like this? Did Dad put something on it, like fertilizer?" one of the boys asked.

"No, I don't think he put anything on it. It started looking like that when he had cancer," said Mrs. Olivia. "That was a beautiful apple tree. Your daddy praised that tree and said his prayers at it, too. He would feel the leaves and branches, and when it started looking shabby, he trimmed it. We got a lot of apples off that tree. You know, God talks about the trees in His Word. I think you all should consult the Lord about this tree and your daddy. He knows all about them both," their mother said, as she stood in the yard with her children.

"I know what we can do!" said the oldest boy. "I'm going to get in touch with everyone tonight and call a meeting. We need all the grands and great grands to come home. These seeds got to leave this house! Mom, if we don't do it this way, you may have problems with this tree later," he said.

Mrs. Olivia told her children to do what they thought was best. She didn't want anything more to do with that apple tree. "I've peeled so many apples, I don't want to see an apple!" she said. "Your daddy loved to plant bushes, flowers and trees. I'd rather work in my house. He always told me that I act like I didn't want anything nice in this house. He was wrong about me. I like flowers, but I like them in a pot. I can take care of them better. He had to keep himself busy outside. I would be in the house washing dishes, and there he goes, off to the store to buy something. I hope you boys don't worry your wives with spending money on your yard. All you need to do is keep the grass cut," their mom said.

CHAPTER 25

The Next Week

A letter was sent to all the siblings. Everyone was to meet at the home on Saturday. The boys were going to have a cook-out for the family. Mrs. Olivia wanted to make a sweet potato pie for her baby girl. She called Minnie. Whenever the children had a cook-out, she always wanted to come.

Saturday Evening

One by one, the children arrived with their families. "Alright, everybody! We need to do a head count. Let's start with the oldest child and work our way down to the baby," said the oldest daughter. She was the secretary for the event. She said, "The oldest brother has eight family members. The oldest girl has 12 family members. The second girl has six family members. The third girl has nine members in her family. The fourth girl has eight family members. The baby girl has three family members. Our deceased brother has six members. The third boy has eleven family members. The fourth boy has six family members and the baby boy has three family members. Is that everybody? Mom let's go outside and say a prayer before we give out the seeds."

Mrs. Olivia went outside with her children. They all made a circle around the tree. She began to pray: *"Father God, who art in Heaven. We come to you this evening giving honor and praise. I want to thank you for taking care of my children on the dangerous highway. Thank you Lord for health and strength. We come to thank you for the head of our home. You knew all about him, Lord, because you made him. Whatever he asked you to do concerning this tree, Lord, do it for us right now. If giving the seeds from his tree gives us a little bit of him back, do it right now, Jesus. If a man dies, shall he live again? He shall live again with you, Lord. From the oldest to the youngest, bless them Lord and bless their seeds. We don't know what tomorrow holds, but you do, Lord. Bless each child that's around this tree. Bless all the parents that are here and anyone who is absent, bless them, also. All these blessings we ask in your precious name. Amen.*

Mr. Will's oldest son opened the bag of seeds. He was surprised to see that his dad had separated the seeds individually. Each bag was labeled with his children's name. The oldest son's bag had 100 seeds in it. He gave everyone their individual little bag. They all opened their bags and they were surprised to see that everybody had 100 seeds.

"What is Daddy trying to tell us? Does this mean that we will be blessed after we are long gone too?" his daughter asked. "100 seeds! If I have four children now, that means that my children will have more children than me and their children will have more than that generation, and so on and so on! I see what he did! He asked the Lord to bless his generation. The seeds from the apple tree represents us, and he is the tree. Daddy has always been a smart man. He did all of this so we will never forget him. I got to keep this going. We need to keep the tree alive within each of us. I'm going to plant my seeds in my back yard when the season permits. I think we all need to do the same thing," she said.

There was not a dry eye in the yard. The baby boy took the surprise harder than the others. All the grandchildren cried on their parent's shoulders. It was like having a funeral all over again.

The children walked their mom back in the house. "Mom, you don't have anything to worry about! If you need groceries or just want to go shopping, give me a call. I can leave the school early and be back home before dark," said her daughter before giving her a kiss. They both walked to the car and said their goodbyes.

The other children left later that night. They talked about what their dad did for them. "I'm telling you man, Daddy got us this time. He had all that planned so well, and we didn't know anything about it. How in the world did he keep that a secret?" asked the baby boy.

"I'm up here every day, almost, and I didn't know about it. He was acting strange after Robert died. If you think about it, after Mr. Tee died, Dad started going down. He seemed to be less active. I thought he was just tired from taking all that medicine. I remembered him telling me that he wasn't afraid to die. I should have thought something then, but I didn't," said the middle boy. All the other children gave their love to their mom and left for home. The calendar was marked to show Mrs. Olivia who was coming next to help her with the house. She had two children to mow her lawn; two to get her grocery; two to clean her house; one to take her shopping and two to take her to church on Sundays.

CHAPTER 26

Four Months Later

I t was hurricane season. The storms were coming every other week. Mrs. Olivia was sitting at her table reading the Bible. Alfonzo, also known as "Al," was walking up the street. He was a good neighbor and a long-time friend of Mr. Will and Mrs. Olivia. He decided to pay Mrs. Olivia a visit. He came up on the porch, and yelled, "Hey, in here! Anybody home?" he asked. "Come on in Al, if your nose is clean," Mrs. Olivia said, as she smiled and met him at the door.

"How are you doing today?" he asked. "You know they're calling for a storm this evening. I can tell by watching the trees," said Mrs. Olivia. "Looks like they are trying to reach up to the Lord. They're swaying from side to side, as if there're going to touch the ground. When they do that, old folks say they're giving the Lord thanks. And you know what? Some people won't thank God for nothing, not even another day of life. The Lord's got more trust in trees and animals than He do in man. I'm going to praise Him while I can. I don't care what they say about me," she said.

Mrs. Olivia sat in her husband's chair and enjoyed talking to her friend. "I believe the storm is turning around. I thought it was going over. You see how dark that cloud is?" she asked Alfonzo. All at once, a loud clap of thunder and lightning came rolling across the house. Alfonzo jumped off the sofa and down to the floor. "What in the world was that?" he shouted, as he crawled on the floor to get under Mrs. Olivia's kitchen table. "My God in Heaven! I thought the sky was falling!" he cried. Mrs. Olivia was laughing so hard she dropped her Bible out of her lap. "Are you alright, Al? We can't hide from the Lord! If he wants us, He knows where we are. My husband would run from room to room, whenever we had a storm. I just sit here and read the Word," said Mrs. Olivia.

Alfonzo raised himself up on one of the kitchen chairs and said, "I got to go home! My hiding place is waiting on me. I go in my closet and close the door. The Bible and everything else can wait. When I was a little boy, my granddaddy would put dark quilts over all our windows. Mom would get in the bed and I would get in with her. They were old and had old ways, but I love those old people. I guess that's why I'm so nervous now," he said, as he got up to looked out the window.

Mrs. Olivia looked out the kitchen window and said, "You see this tree out here? All this rain, and that tree is as solid as a rock. It looks as if it's going to fall to pieces in a minute, but it's not going anywhere until they cut it down."

Alfonzo went to the window to see what she was talking about. "I didn't know that tree looked like that! Mr. Will had a beautiful apple tree. The leaves were so green, and the apples were good. I would come by here and pick some off the ground. He made a lot of money off that tree. Have you ever heard of a tree crying?" he asked Mrs. Olivia.

She looked at him and said, "No! Where did you get that from? The only tree I ever heard of crying was a Weeping Willow tree. People would say that you could see the water falling from a Weeping Willow. I heard my Pa say the one we had in the back yard would weep."

Alfonzo looked a second time, and whispered to Mr. Olivia, "You see what I see? That tree is crying! Look at it! There's something running down the bark! You can see it if you look close enough. What in the world? What's wrong with that tree? It looks dead, but it's not. There's life in a dead tree! I have never seen anything like this in my whole life. I got to get out of here!"

Mrs. Olivia tried to explain what was happening, but Alfonzo didn't stop. He was rushing out the front door. Mrs. Olivia knew there was something wrong with a grown man running from a tree. She went to the door behind him and said, "Al, you be careful. I don't want you to fall down those steps. The tree isn't crying. Trees have sap in them. It looks like water, but it's not. There's nothing wrong with the tree." Alfonzo didn't look back. He walked across the yard and down the hill he went. He waved goodbye and said, "I'll see you next time, Mrs. Olivia."

"Lord, that boy is so scary. There's nothing wrong with that tree," Mrs. Olivia thought. "He came up here running from the lightning, running from the thunder, now running from a tree. Poor Alfonzo! I feel sorry for him. I can't wait to tell the children about him," she said while laughing and opening her Bible to read the Word.

CHAPTER 27

Five Months Later

Mrs. Olivia was doing well. She kept herself busy visiting the elderly, getting her own groceries, paying her bills and writing letters every day to her children. If she didn't receive one back, it was okay, she was going to send them another one.

The weather was getting cooler. She was sitting alone on this dreary day and decided to get up and look out the window. She thought she heard a car! An unfamiliar car pulled into the driveway. It was her two nephews from South Carolina. She was so surprised! "You all come in the house," she told the boys. They came inside and gave her a tight hug.

"We were coming this way and wanted to check on you! We haven't seen you since Will died. You look so good!" they said. "We see that you've been taking care of yourself, too. Have your children been home lately?" the two asked, as they took their seats. Mrs. Olivia offered them something to drink and answered, "No, they work all the time and when they're not traveling, they will come by. I enjoy being by myself. Me and Pa was married for over 50 years. He was wild when we had our first baby, and he didn't get any better when we had the other nine. God is good all the time! I don't know what I would've done without the Lord. I promised Him I would stay with my husband until I die, or whoever left here first, but the Lord took him first."

She continued. "People don't obey the Lord, now. They marry and promise God they're going to stay through sickness or health; good or bad;

give yourself only to your husband or wife; and the first time the husband does something or says something they don't like, they're ready to separate. These young girls don't know nothing about marriage and the young men have to sow their wild oats; that's what old people would say," she told her nephews.

The two boys enjoyed their aunt talking about the good old days, because she was full of wisdom. "We came by for another reason, too. Do you still have apples from your tree?" one of the boys asked, as he looked out the kitchen window. Mrs. Olivia got up and went to her freezer and got a paper bag. "Yes. Pa had so many apples before he passed, we had to freeze them. I have apple pies, sliced apples, apple dumplings, and dried apples. How many bags do you want?" she asked.

They each wanted a pie. Mrs. Olivia put the pies in a bag and gave them to the boys. "Do you need anything, Auntie? We didn't give you anything when Will passed away, so we are going to bless you this day," her nephew said. "We don't want you to say anything, just take what we give you and put it away. Whenever you go with your children, buy yourself something. You were good to us when Momma and Daddy was living. I will never forget how you and Will would come see Momma. She would gain strength when you walked through the door. She loved you like a daughter. We loved to hear her tell us about when she first got married. She said you stayed with them after your mom died. She told us how you took care of us when she had one of her babies. Our parents had a hard time back then. I'm thankful to God that we have made it this far," one of the boys said as he handed Mrs. Olivia $100.

She was surprised. She didn't want to take their money because they had families and their children were in school. She closed her hand with the money in it and said, "Thank you boys so much. I hate to take your money, but Lord, I thank you for all my blessings." The boys got up and gave their auntie one more hug and kiss. It was getting late and they had an hour's drive ahead of them.

The Next Day

The children called early in the morning. The boys wanted to come home and look at the apple tree and clean the yards. The girls were coming to do some cleaning in the house and whatever their mother needed to be done.

Noon

Mrs. Olivia was hanging her clothes on the line. She heard a car. She took her clothes basket and walked around to the front of the house. It was all four of her boys. "Hey Momma! What are you doing out here? It's a little chilly!" one of the boys said.

Mrs. Olivia loved hanging clothes on the line. She grabbed her son and gave him a big hug and said, "My clothes smell better when I hang them on the line. It's not cool, to me! I have on a lot of clothes and they keep me warm. Are you all hungry? I cooked some collards and sweet potatoes this morning."

The boys told her they had eaten on the way. "We are waiting on the girls. They said they were going to be here by noon and it's going on 1 p.m." said her son. "We need to discuss Dad's apple tree. I looked at it when you were outside. It looks bad, Mom. We need to get this yard cleaned up before it gets cold. The girls don't think we should cut it down, but Dad is gone now. We can't allow this yard to look like this. I think that's them pulling up now," said the third son.

Mrs. Olivia met them at the door. "Come in if your nose is clean," she said, as she opened the door and gave them a hug. "Mom, we came to help you around the house and the guys want us to discuss something about the apple tree," said one of the girls. "I don't know what they think we can say or do about Daddy's tree. I thought he told us not to cut the tree down. Is the tree bothering you, Mom? Be honest. Tell us how you feel. If you want the tree down, say so. If not, then, the tree will stay where it is. It's Daddy's tree. He planted that tree for us. I think we should leave it alone," said another daughter.

"I'm going to tell you now! We're not fighting over a tree," said the baby boy. "The men are the ones who keep the yard up and the girls got Mom and inside the house. We share the responsibility around here. So, we are going to vote. There are 10 people here. If there's a tie, then we will draw straws. What do you all say about that?" he asked. Mrs. Olivia kept silent. She let her children make the decision.

"I think we need to cut the tree down. It looks bad near the window. It's bending over," said the oldest son. "It's black and cruddy. It's the worst looking tree on this street. I say cut it down and we're not talking about it anymore. When do you want to come back down here? Let it be on the weekend, because I have to get my rest during the week-days," he said. "Well, I guess this meeting is over!" said the baby boy. "Our oldest brother has spoken. Next Saturday will be the meeting day. What time are we coming? We need to be getting back home before dark," he said.

Everyone said their goodbyes to their mother. Mrs. Olivia went in the house and got her Bible. She always said a prayer before she started reading. *"Lord, I want to thank you for this day. You woke us early this morning and for that you are worthy to be praised. Help my children, Lord! They don't know what to do now that their daddy is gone. They have never been without him. Help them to make the right decisions when it comes to me and this house. They had a good daddy and he took care of his home the best way he knew how. You, Lord, gave us five boys and you took one away. Give the ones you left behind, a heart to consult you before doing anything for this house, for me and even for themselves. Bless my boys and my girls. They are not bad children and we have never had any trouble out of them. While you're passing out blessings tonight, Lord, don't forget the sick, the shut-in, my family, my neighbors, my friends and my enemies. All these blessings I ask in your holy name. Amen.*

She continued to read Psalm 1, in memory of her husband and Psalm 90 for herself. As soon as she finished reading, one of Mr. Will's friends came by. He was the friend who worked on the plumbing. "Knock, knock. Anybody home?" he said as he opened the door. Mrs. Olivia was sitting at the table. She got up and met him at the door.

"Come on in! I thought that was you," she said. "Have a seat." The man sat down for a while and said, "I saw your light on and I decided to stop and check on you. Did I see the boy's cars here today? And I saw a few different cars here, too! Is everything alright?" he asked. "Yes, the children came home to have a meeting about that apple tree," said Mrs. Olivia. "Some want to cut it down and some don't. I don't care what they do. I'm not going to be here long, anyway. I'll be gone and that tree will be here. I know you're glad your parents didn't have all of this to deal with. When you have a lot of children, that's a lot of talk going on. Some want this. Some want that. What the oldest say, what the baby says, it can go on and on," she said to her friend.

"Well, I tell you! Mr. Will was a man who knew what he wanted," said her friend. "He was smart, too! You couldn't fool him. If you tried, he would make a fool out of you! You couldn't cheat him either. I really miss that man. If, he was here they wouldn't talk long, because he would do all the talking. Will was like a father to me. Did I ever tell you that he was the one who help me stop drinking? We had a long talk one day near the apple tree. He told me about the time he was in the Navy. He said when he came back home, he would drink a lot. He said he was like a crazy man! That liquor was like the devil himself coming out of him. It frightened me! When he told me that, I thought about how I acted when I get too much. I don't want people to be afraid of me. I love people and I want them to love me. Like you and your husband. I been knowing you all for a long time. I think one of your boys was in my class. But when I started working on this house for Mr. Will, I found a friend for life. Be sure to tell those boys to make the right decision. They act like Mr. Will—tell them to think like him, too," he said as he got up and headed for the door. Mrs. Olivia thanked him for coming by and told him to stop by anytime.

CHAPTER 28

The Next Weekend

Mrs. Olivia had a good week. She was preparing dinner for her children. They all were coming at 2 p.m. to cut down the tree. They all arrived at the same time! Mrs. Olivia was sitting at the table. She said, "You all gather around the table so we can have a word of prayer. We don't want to do anything before we consult the Lord. I feel good about what's going to happen. Your daddy is gone on to Heaven. We need to thank the Lord one more time before you bury the tree."

She began to pray. *"I thank you Lord, I thank you for this day. Have mercy on us! Thank you for all my children, Lord. Thank you for what you have given us down through the years. You put food on our table. You put shoes on our feet. You, Lord did the healing when we were sick. You died for us all on the cross and forgave our sins. For all of that I want to say, 'thank you.' Now, Lord, this tree that my husband prayed over, thank you for it. Release it back to the earth from which it came, just like you released my husband from this evil world! Let the seeds from this tree remind the generations to come many years after us, to never forget Will. I'm praying to you, Lord, in the name of the Father, the Son and the Holy Spirit. Amen."*

"Who said we were going to bury daddy's tree? I thought you boys were going to cut it down and throw it in the woods across the street," said one of the girls. "If Mom wants us to bury it, then, we will bury the tree. It doesn't matter, bury or burn, we got to rid of it. I want to know, who's going to do the cutting and what are you going to cut it with?" said the baby boy.

The boys looked around at each other. "Did anyone bring an ax or a saw?" someone asked. Mrs. Olivia walked to her bedroom. She had the key to the storage barn. Mr. Will kept all his tools in the storage, so maybe he had an ax or saw in there, also. "Here, take this key and see if your daddy has something to cut it with. I think he had a saw out there. If there is one in there, you need to oil it, and be careful not to hurt yourself," Mrs. Olivia said.

The oldest boy went to the storage. When he opened it, there was a saw and an ax in the corner of the building. He got them both. He laid the ax near the tree and gave the saw to the baby boy. They all gathered around the tree. "Who's going to do the cutting?" asked the baby boy. "Well, since we don't have any volunteers, I guess I will have the pleasure! You all get back! Tell the girls if they don't want to see this, stay in the house with Momma. We don't want any crying out here. You all know what Daddy would say. 'Everything that lives must die.' This tree lived for many years, now it must be put to rest. Alright! Here goes!" he said.

As soon as he was about to turn the saw on, one of the girls was standing in the window. She screamed, "Oh, my daddy!" The baby boy looked up and saw her, and yelled, "Somebody, go in there and shut her mouth. Hurry up! I can't stand all of that hollering! She should've stayed home. Tell her to go get in the closet or hide under the bed! She is making me nervous."

The oldest boy went in the house and told his sister that everything was going to be alright. "Go in the bedroom and hide in the closet. We all are going to miss the tree," he said.

After their sister was calmed, they continued to cut down the tree. When he started cutting the tree, he cut it from the top—limb by limb! He cut small branches, then the larger branches. Finally, he cut the trunk in half. Then, he trimmed the other half of the trunk. But, when he cut the bottom half, the tree came alive again.

"Do you all see what I see? This tree isn't dead all the way through," the baby boy said. "It looks dead on the outside, but inside is beautiful. I believe this is the soul of this tree. This tree is just like us; it has a body, a soul and a spirit. The body was corrupted—sinful, ugly on the outside. It went through a lot in its lifetime. The soul is that part that we see now. When I cut the trunk in half, its color changed, it has renewed itself. And the spirit of this tree will live forever in us. That's what Daddy was trying to tell us. That's why he did what he did. He knew this tree would never die. Just like us. If we live a good and productive life; do what the Lord wants us to do; read our Bible like Daddy did; help others, love people and not do others wrong; we will be like a tree planted by the rivers of water. I got it now! It took me a long time to figure this out, but I see what he was doing for us. We are going to bury the dead part of this tree. I want to cover it with the dirt from the earth. And the soul part of the tree...we are going to leave it the way it is. God will do the rest," he said.

All the boys cleaned the back yard. The tree branches and limbs were buried across the road from their house. Mrs. Olivia was sad about the way her daughter reacted. She knew how some of her children felt about their daddy. They all loved him, but they all didn't understand death. She had told them over and over again. "We got to leave here. We can't stay!"

All the children were ready to go back to their homes. Mrs. Olivia was standing in the door watching the cars leave the driveway. She loved all her children, but she loved being home alone with just her and the Lord too.

CHAPTER 29

The Next Week

One of her favorite neighbors was coming up the street. He walked up the hill to Mrs. Olivia's house. "Hey in here! Anybody home?" he yelled. Mrs. Olivia saw him coming, so she got up to unlock the door and said, "Hey Alfonzo! Come on in the house and have some coffee water." He stepped inside and said, "Coffee water! What is that?" Mrs. Olivia smiled while sipping out of her cup and answered him, "It's hot sugar water with a sprinkle of coffee. I can't drink my coffee black like Pa did. He would have so much coffee in his cup, it looked like syrup. Do you want a cup?" she asked.

Alfonzo looked around the room to find a seat and said, "I like my coffee the way I like my women—black and sweet. I don't mean no harm, but that's the way I am." They both had a good laugh. Alfonzo laughed so hard; he almost fell out of his chair. He stood and walked over to the kitchen window and said, "You know, I was walking up the road, and things didn't look right in your back yard. They cut that apple tree down! When did that happen!? It makes this whole lot look different. It looks like somebody is dead for real, now."

Mrs. Olivia smiled at Alfonzo and said, "Somebody is dead for real—my Pa!" Alfonzo laughed. "I tell you one thing, and I don't care who knows it," Alfonzo said. "That was a scary tree! I will never forget when I saw that tree cry. You said it was weeping. I know the difference between weeping and crying. That tree was crying like a baby. If God can make a jackass talk to a foolish man, he can make a tree cry real tears. Now that's the way I see it. What you think about that?" he asked Mrs. Olivia. She smiled and said, "The only thing I know is, God is God! This is his world. He rules and regulates it. No man can do these things. No man can put breath in us, and no man can make the sun shine by day and the noon by night. He woke me up this morning and he started me on my way. For that, all I can say is, Lord, I thank you!" Alfonzo stayed for a while chatting with Mrs. Olivia. They were good friends and neighbors. All her friends and family would visit every week.

Mrs. Olivia lived in her home until her health failed her. Mr. Will was 80 years old when he died, and she lived nine more years after his death.

The soul of the apple tree is still in the back yard of their home. Her favorite scripture, Psalm 90, will live in her children's hearts forever:

"Lord, you have been our dwelling place throughout all generations. Before the mountains were born or you brought forth the whole world, from everlasting to everlasting you are God. You turn people back to dust, saying, 'Return to dust, you mortals.' A thousand years in your sight are like a day that has just gone by, or like a watch in the night. Yet you sweep people away in the sleep of death—they are like the new grass of the morning: In the morning it springs up new, but by evening it is dry and withered. We are consumed by your anger and terrified by your indignation. You have set our iniquities before you, our secret sins in the light of your presence. All our days pass away under your wrath; we finish our years with a moan. Our days may come to seventy years, or eighty, if our strength endures; yet the best of them are but trouble and sorrow, for they quickly pass, and we fly away."

FAMILY & FRIENDS

MR. WILL & MRS. OLIVIA

RAY ANTHONY, MR. WILL & MRS. OLIVA'S SON WHO DIED

MR. WILL & HIS FRIEND, MR. CHAVIS

THE BOYS CUT DOWN THE APPLE TREE

ON MAY 30, 2020